SAGI

JOHN WEGENER

SAGI

Written by John Wegener.
Published by Prosolin.
Copyright © 2022 John Wegener.
Copyright © 2022 Cover designed by Fiona Jayde Media.

1

CLUBBING

I COMBED BACK my dark-brown hair. The large mirror reflected a clean-shaven face and eyes sparkling with excitement. I stepped backward to check my appearance. My clothes hung on me with no special allure that I could see — but then, I didn't know what women found alluring. I wore a pale-blue shirt that subtly complemented my darker blue eyes, and the black slimline pants fitted snugly on my legs, thanks to the mandated, age-appropriate exercise routine we all had to do in our apartments every day. Black canvas shoes completed the outfit for my night of clubbing with my friends. I put the comb away and took a deep breath to ease my stomach flutters. I was ready. With another dreary week alone in the apartment over, I was looking forward to getting out, so to speak.

I turned and walked over to the PR room. This room (full name the 'Personal Reality' room) was an essential part of every person's apartment. It comprised a chair and headset where one sat and connected with the World Neural Network (or WNN, as everyone called it). When directly connected to your brain, WNN allowed personal interaction as if in real life. A wraparound section covered the rest of the body, which provided feed for touch. Other sections input sight, hearing, taste, and smell. You couldn't tell the difference between it and reality — or so everyone said.

I sat in the chair and took more calming breaths, as I didn't want my friends to notice my nervousness. I was always like this before going clubbing. It was because the mere thought of talking to girls terrified me. My friend Jason didn't have a nervous bone in his body, but for me, the sight of an attractive girl, or indeed any girl, always rendered me tongue-tied. How was I ever going to meet the woman of my dreams when I always sounded so pathetic?

Once I dialed the destination, I pressed the activate button.

Lights lit up, and the head cap rotated into position and lowered onto my skull. A mask wrapped around my nose and mouth, the cylinder encircled my body, and tendrils enveloped every part of me. I wriggled to get comfortable and waited ...

———

"Hey, Ossy, what took you so long?" Jason shouted as he saw me approach him through the club's entrance.

Loud thumping music blared as multi-colored lights flashed in synchronous rhythm. People crowded the premises, a few dancing, others crushed at the bar, and still others seated in tables distributed beside the dance floor. Most stood in the gaps, watching the interaction of humanity around them. Jason was a member of the standing crowd, as were several others with him. I walked up to them. "Whoa, Jason," I replied. "Good to see ya. I got held up with a last-minute design change. But I'm here now. Let's party."

"Woo-hoo, let's do it." Jason waved his arms above his head.

"Yeah," the others shouted.

I greeted each of them, friends I had met over the years. A few were familiar, others not so close, and none as solid as Jason. After gaining a server's attention and ordering a beer, I scanned the room to find other acquaintances. "Been here long?"

"Ten, fifteen minutes," Jason replied.

"How's it looking tonight?"

"Bit early to tell. Still plenty coming in, so it should end up a wild night." Jason nudged me suggestively.

I tingled with excitement as I snickered at Jason's gesture. My drink came, and I took a gulp, pleased at how the alcohol instantly started calming my nerves. Just how it could do that when this was PR and not reality, I didn't know and didn't question.

I liked Jason. He just flowed with the motion of events without thinking of the consequences, sometimes getting us both into outlandish and awkward spots. We would laugh at it afterward, wondering how we got into such predicaments — or at least, he would wonder. I always knew that it was Jason that got us there.

"Hey, see her?" Jason prodded.

"Where?"

"Over there. The one with the red sequined dress. She looks lonely, Ossy."

"Oh, I don't know. I'm sure she has a date coming to meet her. Someone as good-looking as her."

"Oh, come on, Ossy. Hasn't stopped you in the past. She's yours. I can sense it."

Fear knotted my stomach as I stared. While I was still mustering the courage to introduce myself, she looked my way as if she sensed my gaze. A smile flashed across her face just as I looked away, embarrassed.

"Come on — she just smiled at you. You've got her."

"Stop it. I'm not ready yet. And get that look off your face."

Jason feigned surprise. "What look?"

"That 'I'm going to have fun at Oswald's expense' expression."

"I'd never do that." Jason looked shocked.

"Yeah, right? Let's just relax."

"Let's nudge closer. Won't hurt."

Against my better judgment, I allowed Jason to draw me nearer to her, taking furtive glances at her all the while and noticing that she was doing the same. I didn't understand why she was standing on her own.

We were getting too near her for comfort, and I had started telling Jason just that when he shoved me right into her, spilling her drink over me and mine onto the floor. I threw my hand out to stop falling over, grabbing the woman's upper arm, and she wrapped her other arm around my neck and chest. As I rebalanced, I straightened, my beet-root-red face radiating embarrassment and heat. "I'm so sorry. I didn't mean ... I mean, I didn't intend ... I mean ..."

As I recovered from the shock, I saw her grin. "Don't worry. I know what your friend did."

I stared at her. She had the most enchanting, husky, contralto voice. I gulped and came out of my trance moments later. "Yeah, he's a jerk." I looked around for Jason, but he was nowhere in sight. I frowned and became irate. "Wait till I see him again."

She laughed and pointed. "He's hiding in the corner over there enjoying his little prank."

I glanced in that direction and gave an angry gesture before returning my attention to her. "He'll be scared to face me for a while."

The woman peered at me as though fascinated, though it beat me why she would find me fascinating. She held her glass to her cheek and swayed from side to side as she studied me. "I'm Rebecca," she said finally.

"Oh ... um ... I'm Oswald, although *friends* call me Ossy." I glanced back at Jason.

"That's an impressive name. Are you a powerful king?"

"Uh?"

She smiled. "That's what 'Oswald' means ... Sorry about the drink."

"Wasn't your fault." I panicked. "I didn't get any on you, did I?"

She smiled. "No, but I'll need another."

"Should make him pay for fresh ones."

A sudden glitter flashed in her eyes. "Don't worry, he will. By the end of the night."

Not understanding what Rebecca meant, I gave her a nervous smile. "Um ... you want me to buy you a new one?"

"Later. Let's dance first."

I gulped. "I don't dance."

"It's easy. Come on," Rebecca said as she grabbed my hand and led me to the dance floor.

With no alternative if I wished to continue my association with her, which I did, I accompanied her. *I'll get Jason big time for this when I catch up with him. Although if it turns out OK, maybe I'll be thanking him ...*

Rebecca let go and started swaying in rhythm to the music, and I tried to copy her. I had a clumsy dancing style at first and wanted to run, but I soon became familiar with the motion and enjoyed cavorting in synchronicity with Rebecca, smiling at her when she looked at me. We stopped and left the floor several songs later. I puffed with exhaustion but followed her, exhilarated, as she led me to an empty table with a long semi-circular couch and sat. I joined her.

"Told you it was easy."

"It's easy when I follow your moves."

She smiled, a sparkle in her eyes. "I'd love that drink now?"

"Oh, sure." After waving in the air, I got the server's attention and ordered two.

Rebecca waved into the crowd moments later, and I craned my neck to see whose attention she wanted. Another woman, searching the club, spotted Rebecca, walked over to us, and said to Rebecca, "Hi. Sorry I'm late — but I see you found yourself some company."

"Hi, Mandy. This is Ossy."

Mandy checked me over with her eyes as she greeted me, and then turned back to Rebecca with a cheeky, "How d'you pick him up so quick?"

"He fell in my lap."

"What?"

Rebecca laughed. "His *friend* decided he should meet me. Sort of behavior I'd attribute to one of my friends."

Mandy chewed gum and looked at Rebecca with mischief. "Who'd that be?"

"You know her."

"Oh, where is this friend?" Mandy asked, changing the subject.

"Ossy, where'd your friend go?"

"I don't know," I said as I scanned the room for Jason. "He must be still hiding." I frowned. *How will I entertain two women? I have enough trouble talking with one.* I fidgeted, still searching the crowd to spot him, finally spying him skulking at the bar. Despite my efforts to grab his attention, he kept looking the other way.

"So, Ossy — you want a threesome?" Mandy asked.

"What?" I spurted out in alarm.

"Stop it," Rebecca said, giggling in her husky voice. "You find your own."

"Oh, just teasing. I thought it might entice your friend over here if he saw your success."

I laughed. "That'd impress him."

Jason, at last, glanced in our direction, and I waved him over.

As he swaggered across the floor with his drink, he cast his eye over Mandy.

Noticing, Mandy said, "You looking at something?"

"Just wondering how Ossy here latched onto two girls so fast."

"He has charm, so find your own girl."

Jason opened his mouth to speak but closed it again, frowning.

Mandy burst out laughing. I smiled too, as did Rebecca, as she wrapped her arm around me and moved in closer. My smile morphed into a nervous twitch. Jason beamed a grin and looked at me. "Well, it worked, didn't it?"

"No thanks to you. I got drink spilled over me."

He shrugged. "Sorry. It was harder than I meant. You going to introduce me, or what?"

"This is Rebecca and Mandy," I said, pointing to each in turn. "And here's Jason, the jerk."

"Hey, no need for that." Jason smiled regardless.

"You deserve it."

"Well, he should get along with Mandy."

"What?" Mandy said, glaring at Rebecca.

"Is that so?" Jason looked at Mandy with greater interest, a more seductive smile.

As she looked back at Jason, Mandy rolled her eyes. "Come over here then, Jerk." She put her hand over her mouth. "Oh ... sorry, Jason. That just slipped out."

After another swift frown, Jason regained his swagger and sat next to her.

Rebecca turned to whisper in my ear, "Told you they'd get on together."

I blushed as I felt her minty breath float across my neck and face, my skin tingling with sensuality as I inhaled it. I gulped, sensing arousal, and nodded as I gazed at her. She watched me with interest. "Everyone right for drinks?" I asked to change the conversation to something less intimidating.

Rebecca drew back but maintained her caress on my arm. The others said they were, and the discussion continued, although Mandy and Jason talked most, which suited me.

"Let's dance again." Rebecca pulled me from the couch. I grimaced but let her lead me to the floor. "We can talk more without those two interfering every second word."

I smiled. "Jason likes to give his opinion."

"As does Mandy. Sparks might fly if they disagree."

I chuckled. "Yeah, that'd be something to watch."

We reached the center of the floor, where Rebecca released me to sway in rhythm to the music; I matched her moves as I had learned to do earlier. I enjoyed dancing with her. Her movements were so easy to follow. The loud blaring song finished and a slower tune came on, bringing Rebecca near me, her arms wrapping around my neck as we danced with more intimacy. I floundered, not sure what to do with my arms but ended up placing them on her hips, which drew her closer to me still. We touched front on, and she stayed in contact, forcing me to wrap my arms around her waist. I blushed as I felt something grow below and looked aside, embarrassed. I sensed her gazing straight at me but couldn't bear to meet her eyes.

She grabbed my chin and turned my head to face hers. "It's OK. Relax. I'm interested in you." Her hand returned to my neck, and she placed her head on my shoulder as she swayed to the slow, pulsing music.

Taking her advice, I joined her rhythmic motion, my embarrassment lessening after a while. *How could such a chance meeting get me in touch with someone so charming?* I thought as I enjoyed her warmth. She lifted her head and stared into my eyes, bringing her mouth to mine, kissing me with the slightest of pressure and returning to her earlier position, leaving me wondering if I had dreamed it. The warmth lingered on my lips. We remained in the slow swaying dance for another two songs before retiring to our seat, Rebecca placing her arm around my waist and her head on my shoulder, as my head stayed light with ecstasy.

The entertainment continued until well after midnight, with Rebecca staying with me the whole time. People started leaving toward one in the morning, and I considered doing likewise, though I was reluctant to leave Rebecca. I was in a bind — the thought of asking her to my place frightened me.

As if knowing what I was thinking, Rebecca reached over and kissed me on the neck, sending a spark of energy through my body. "Want to come back home with me?" she whispered in my ear as her breath teased my lobe. I looked at her and nodded. We said goodbye to Jason and Mandy and left.

2

IN THE OPEN

AFTER WAKING QUITE LATE the next morning, I sat up in bed and stretched, smiling as I remembered my time with Rebecca after we'd left the club. I had never met anyone as intriguing as her, so forward and sensuous and yet honest and shy at the same time, as we talked and increased our intimacy. My head throbbed with a hangover, so I flopped back and dozed before gaining enough energy to rouse myself.

Wondering what I should do with my day off, I looked at the calendar in my display, and my eyes widened as I remembered my outer was due (officially known as the Allocated Monthly Hour Outside) — an event to relish. How could I have forgotten that? The encounter with Rebecca had driven even it from my mind.

"You have an incoming call from Jason," my communication interface announced.

I groaned as I knew what the prime topic of conversation would be. "Accept with visual."

Jason's image lit up the screen moments later. "Hey, lover boy. How you doing?"

"Yeah, fine."

"So, you scored."

"None of your business. What did you do afterward?"

"Oh, nothing much. We stayed a while longer and left. Got her contact details, though."

"You going to get in touch?"

"Might. You must have had a good night. Looks like you just woke."

"Again, none of your business. Stop being such a busybody."

Jason grinned. "Just checking up on my handiwork. Told you she was hot."

I rolled my eyes and walked off to grab a drink. The image levitated from its resting spot on the screen and followed me. "Well, I didn't need the not so gentle shove. They'll charge extra to get the stain out of my shirt." I poured a glass of juice.

"I said I was sorry. Anyway, what's happening? Want to hang out?"

"Not today. Got my outer this afternoon."

"Yeah? Lucky you. Wish mine was due. Might see you next Friday, then? Or you got other plans?" Jason peered at me with a cheeky grin.

Blushing, I mumbled, "No, nothing's arranged. We'll decide when Friday gets closer."

"Catch you then." The image vanished before I could reply.

I shook my head. *Typical*, I whispered to myself.

"End call," I said to the screen, and the interface turned off.

After finishing the drink, I made cereal and fruit and sat at the table, eating. It was ten-thirty. I had nothing special to do to amuse myself until two, the scheduled time of my AMHO. My mind wandered, and I started reminiscing about the night with Rebecca again. For the first time, my shyness with women had not been a handicap. She seemed to like my shyness. Her personality was so forthright and outgoing that it balanced mine perfectly. I wondered if we could have a fulfilling relationship. We were still young. No one else my age had settled into a commitment yet. I had plenty of time. *It isn't often I meet someone like Rebecca, though. Have I stumbled on the person to commit to?* I had her contact details. I might tempt her with dinner or a holo-movie. *What if she wasn't interested and just wanted a casual contact? How embarrassing if she didn't want something more.* I sighed. Too much thinking.

I showered and looked at the weather forecast for outside before selecting suitable clothing. It predicted a warm sunny day with little wind, so I put on a black tee-shirt and my favorite faded blue jeans, setting aside a jacket, just in case. Bored waiting, I scrolled through the local news on the interface. Rebecca's contact flashed in the screen's corner for me to accept, distracting me. I tried ignoring it, as I didn't want her to think me too eager. With self-reproach, I sat back. *You idiot. You know she's great. Acknowledge the damn thing.* I tapped the flashing spot, and her details appeared. After another tap, it stopped. I continued my scrolling.

"You have an incoming call from Rebecca."

I froze and gulped as I stared at the screen. I couldn't move, couldn't respond.

"You have an incoming call from Rebecca."

I shook myself from my self-imposed stupor. "Accept with visual."

Rebecca's face flashed on the screen, her cheery smile complementing her symmetrical facial features. *How does she make herself so gorgeous with so little sleep?*

"Hi, sleepyhead," she said.

My cheeks ignited into radiating heat. "Hi. Wasn't expecting you to call so soon."

"I've been sitting here waiting for you to acknowledge my contacts for ages." She gave a cheeky smile.

"Oh, sorry. Didn't mean to make you wait. I only just woke up."

She laughed in her husky contralto voice, sending shivers up my spine. "I'm joking. The acknowledgment flashed, so I thought I'd give you a quick call, see how you recovered."

"I'm fine. Bit of a headache. Shouldn't have drunk so much. You look fantastic."

"Oh ... thanks." Rebecca blushed and glanced away. I hadn't seen her blush before, and it made her look cute. It highlighted her high cheekbones and gave me another shiver. "What you doing today?"

"I've got my outer soon. Just lazing otherwise."

"Oh."

She looked disappointed as if she wanted to meet again straight away. "You want to get together tonight?" I asked.

Her disappointment intensified. "I can't. Doing something."

It was my turn for regret. "When are you free, then? I have a dull life apart from programming."

She frowned and looked at another part of her screen. "Night after next?"

"Good. Want a bite to eat?"

"Sure. Meet at Sylvester's at seven?"

"Is that in the mega-mall on the sixth level?"

"Yeah."

"Oh ... yeah, OK. I've never been there."

"You'll enjoy it. Full of nerds."

I jerked back and smiled. "Who said I'm a nerd?"

"You're a software engineer, aren't you?"

"Yeah."

"You're a nerd."

"Thanks a lot." I laughed.

Rebecca grinned back at me.

"OK then. I'd better go. See you then."

"Yeah." The screen blanked.

"End call." The display returned to my earlier page. I reclined in ecstasy as my heart pounded. *Wow. She'd called me.* And now I had two things to look forward to: my outer and her.

Not knowing what else to do while I waited for two o'clock to come round, I tidied my bedroom and ate a sandwich.

Right on the dot of two I heard my exit door unlock. I stared at it, nervous it wouldn't open, but when I placed my hand in the indentation, it slid open, revealing the complex's corridor on my floor. My exit door was a replica of every other exit door in my apartment complex, housing other individuals, I presumed, who had their own outer time different from mine. I had never once since any of those doors open.

I dashed along the passageway, entered the elevator, and descended to ground level. I wondered how high I lived. No number designated the floor I lived on, but the elevator always ferried me to the correct spot when I returned. From observation, I judged less than two hundred lived in the complex based on its size outside — but looks can be deceptive. I had never circumnavigated the building. After erasing the distracting thought, I rocked from foot to foot in anticipation, my hands in my pockets. The elevator doors opened, and I entered the foyer. A click sounded when I placed my right hand over the identification pad, and the outer doors slid open. My hour had started.

A warm breeze blew across my face as I stepped outside and strolled into the landscape, mesmerizing me as always with a charm that somehow PR could never quite replicate. A path led away from the building into the parklands surrounding the complex. As I ambled along it, I enjoyed the serenity of what I heard and saw. A bird, out of sight, sang. Trees swayed, their leaves projecting scintillating spots of light on the ground as they fluttered. The soil's earthiness and composting vegetation tantalized my nostrils. When I came to the end of the tree line and gazed out, a large lake dominated my view with short grass extending a verge between the woods and the shore. A bench seat stood nearby where I liked to sit. I walked over to it and sat as I absorbed the vista of the lake and the hills behind it, with their verdant expanse shining in the sunlight.

Just think. This is real, not a projected reality. I frowned. *How do I know it isn't a projected reality? Is there any distinction? Everything looks, sounds, tastes, and feels the same, so how do I know it's different? We're told this reality is the real one — but is it? Is there a subtle difference I didn't notice before, something so innocuous that no one notices it? It doesn't matter. It seems physical, and I only get to experience it once a month, so enjoy your hour.*

A deer strolled out from the trees a hundred yards away. My jaw dropped. I had never seen a deer in real life. It was brown with mottled white spots and a fawn-colored belly. It lowered its head as it nibbled off blades of grass, heading toward the lake, not noticing me sitting nearby. I was downwind, so the deer didn't smell me either. I sat fascinated by the animal as it meandered toward the water and started drinking. Its head darted up, smelling the air, fidgeting. A large cat raced out of the trees, headed for the deer. Startled and frightened, the deer bolted into a gallop straight toward me, its eyes frenzied in fear, as were mine. The feline closed the gap as the deer sped past me. Catching the deer two hundred yards further on, the cat pounced onto it and wrestled it to the ground, its massive jaws clamping into the prey's neck as it crushed its windpipe, biting into the flesh. The deer lashed and jerked to escape, but its motion slowed after a time and stopped soon afterward. The cat stood up with the deer's neck still in its mouth, blood dripping from its exposed teeth, searching for other predators or scavengers that might challenge it for its catch. It locked its eyes on me for an instant before looking away, a sixth sense telling it I was no threat.

I gulped in fear, not knowing if the cat might switch its interest to me after eating the deer. *Surely it couldn't eat the whole deer and still be hungry.* I watched the cat drag the deer out of sight as my heart slowed its pounding. I scanned nearby, but any other animals had deserted the place — although I hadn't noticed the deer and cat before they broke into the open, either. How many creatures prowled without being seen? I realized I lacked preparation for such an eventuality. I had no weapons of self-defense. No one required any.

I needed to go somewhere else. Cautiously, I stood, scanning my surroundings, and slinked to the lake. A modest wooden jetty jutted from the shoreline that I liked to visit. Sometimes the weather didn't allow it. I strolled over to the anchor point and started along the projection, my footsteps plodding on the boards, breaking the tranquil silence. When I reached the end, I sat with my legs dangling over the side. I felt at peace again as I looked at the sun's reflection on the myriad ripples racing across the water's surface. The clear water provided a view into its depths. Small fish darted out from under the pier, weaving their way around the piles. I swung my legs back and forth as I watched. I wished Rebecca was with me to experience this tranquility and wondered why I met no one outside. As I returned my gaze to the horizon, I tried to spot any changes from last time but couldn't. Time elapsed as I rested and absorbed the serenity of my surroundings.

The timer beeped at me from my wrist, warning me of five minutes to go before I must return to my apartment for another month. I silenced it and sighed. Reluctantly, I rose to my feet, peered out across the lake one last time, and returned indoors.

3

A BABY

THE CODING on the screen stumped me as I dissected the lines. A problem existed, but I couldn't find it, grinding my teeth in frustration. To get paid, I had to submit the design today, but it had to work or they'd throw it back at me, whoever 'they' were. My script was part of a larger routine for a new mall complex in the PR space. I didn't know where they intended to use it. They didn't give me that sort of information when they gave me the assignments, only the feed information and the output requirements. I don't recall ever seeing reality structures I could pinpoint as my work when I entered the PR space, but I wasn't sure if I could tell, anyway. It was late afternoon, and the pressure to finish weighed on me as time elapsed. Grunting in irritation, I stood and went to pour a drink as the symbols rolled through my mind.

"Incoming call from Cynthia."

Wonder what she wants, I thought, erasing the remnants of my problem. "Accept on visual." An ecstatic face appeared on the screen. "Hi, sis. What's happening?"

"You'll never guess what. Rory and I are getting a baby."

"What? That's great. How did that happen?" I bubbled over, elated by her announcement. She and her husband Rory had been applying to the nursery authority for years without success.

"Isn't it incredible? I can't wait. Oh, it'll be fantastic." Cynthia jumped around, tears threatening to erupt.

"Hey. I want to visit. Can I? You can tell me the rest when I arrive."

"Sure, come over now. I can't wait."

I hung up and gazed in despair at my work but decided it could wait an hour. A break to take my mind off it might help me resolve the issue when I returned. My sister's news filled me with joy. She looked so happy. After tidying myself up, I rushed to my PR room and dialed Cynthia's residence before sitting in the chair and pressing the button.

———

As I knocked on Cynthia's door, the sound of knocking reverberated and a knuckle-on-wood sensation flowed up my arm. The door flung open.

"Come in, Oswald, quick! I'll tell you everything."

I beamed as I crossed the threshold, excited by her excitement. Cynthia closed the door and pulled me through into the living room. "Whoa, whoa. Slow down. You're hurting me."

"I'm sorry. I'm so excited. You want a drink?"

"A beer if you've got one."

"Sure." Cynthia disappeared into the kitchen and returned moments later with a bottle and glass. "Sit. Here's your beer." She filled the glass and placed both on a side table near a lounge chair where I'd parked myself.

I took a sip. "Now tell me the news. When did you find out?"

Cynthia sat opposite me and leaned forward. "Just before I rang you. Well, I called Mom and Dad first. They're over the moon. Mom's busy thinking of everything she can give it." She rolled her eyes.

I chuckled. Mom wanted a grandchild almost as much as Cynthia and Rory wanted a child. The procedure wasn't that simple, though. "So, what happened?"

"Well, I'd finished work for the day and had started making something to eat when the nursery authority called. They said they had accepted our application for a baby this time. Oh, it's taken so long. And we still have to wait. There's a queue, so we must wait another two months before ours becomes available. But we're getting one. We're getting one, Ossy!"

"I'm so happy for you, sis. What's Rory say?"

Cynthia rolled her eyes again. "He's more excited than me." She giggled. "He's wondering if it'll be a girl or a boy. They haven't said yet. And he's chasing up what standard of nursery room and carer-bot we can afford. He wants the biggest and the best for his little baby, but I suppose we'll return to reality. We're not millionaires. But he says there are some excellently priced rooms becoming available that look great. We're going to look at them on our next recreation day. And the carer-bots are reasonably priced, too." As babies resided in nurseries until they grew old enough for a unit of their own, they had carer-bots to look after them when the child's parents weren't with them in PR. I still vaguely remember mine with sadness. My life changed when I moved to my unit.

I sat back. "Wow! My sister a mom. That'll take some getting used to."

"Oh, Ossy, it'll just seem like I've always been a mother before long."

I daydreamed. "And I'll be an uncle."

Cynthia beamed. "Yes. You want to stay for dinner?"

I grimaced. "I'd love to, but I've got a design I have to send today, and it's being a pain in the neck. I thought taking a break might help, but I'd better get back and finish it."

"Next time, then. Hey, the grapevine says you've got a girlfriend."

"Where'd you hear that?" I turned bright red.

"So, it's true."

"Maybe. We've only just met. Met her at a club. But we do have a date this week ..."

"Do Mom and Dad know?"

"No, and don't tell them. I'll kill you if you tell them."

Cynthia laughed. "Oh, Mom will be so happy. Her little boy all grown up and with a girlfriend."

"Stop teasing."

"Isn't that what sisters do?"

"No."

"Well, is she nice?"

"*Of course* she's nice. I wouldn't be going out with her if she wasn't nice."

"What's her name?"

I started moving around in the chair, trying to find a more comfortable spot to soothe my current discomfort. "Rebecca. It's early days yet."

Cynthia grinned at me but remained silent.

"Well, I must go. And it's great news about the baby. I'm so happy for you and Rory." I stood and finished the beer. Once I'd disposed of the bottle and glass, I returned to her to say goodbye.

"We'll organize a date for you to visit for dinner."

"Yeah."

"You can bring Rebecca," she added with a cheeky grin.

"Stop it," I replied, but I grinned back. "See you later." I reached over and kissed her on the cheek.

"Bye."

I left through the door.

———

I stretched as I stood up from the PR chair. Cynthia's news had made me happy. She and Rory had waited years for a baby. And now they were receiving one. Sighing, I returned to the living room and stared at the display with the computer code still glowing its disdain at me and sighed again. I sat and stared at the screen, getting no more inspiration. One line drew attention to itself, though, but I couldn't understand why. *You idiot. How didn't you see that?* I found the error and changed the code, running it in simulation afterward. It ran to perfection, which gave me a smile at last. I packaged it and sent it off to finish my work for the day, elated. That should get a good payout.

"You have an incoming call from Jason."

I frowned. Jason never called so late. "Accept call with visual."

Jason's face appeared on the screen. He looked serious and upset. "What's wrong?"

"Turn on your news feed."

"Why?"

"Just turn it on," Jason snapped.

I looked at him, perturbed by his manner. "OK." I tapped on the news space of the screen and looked at it. "And?"

"Scroll down."

I did as he instructed and flipped through the current news items until Rebecca's face appeared. I gasped. "What's this?" I opened the story and started reading it. *That's not possible.* "She's dead?" I looked back at Jason.

Jason looked at me with concern. "Looks that way."

"But how? People our age don't die. I never heard of someone our age dying." The news flattened me. She was so outgoing and bubbly. The room brightened whenever she entered it. I started fiddling with my hands to distract myself.

"You OK?"

"Not really. You know I liked her."

"Yeah, I know. It doesn't say how she died. They just say natural causes. Want me to come over on PR?"

I heaved. "No, it's OK." I avoided eye contact with Jason for fear of crying. "I want to be alone. See you soon." I ended the call. It couldn't be right. I gave Rebecca a call, convinced she'd answer it, proving the story a fake. Maybe a case of mistaken identity. I tapped her contact and waited.

"This contact is no longer connected."

It wasn't a nightmare then. It was real. *Rebecca is dead.* I knew I'd barely known her, but the news had a devastating effect on me, nonetheless. Our future together had seemed so promising, but now fate had snuffed out the flame in an instant. My own life suddenly seemed immensely empty.

4

AN ENCOUNTER

I FELL into a haze of misery after Rebecca died. Jason struggled to cheer me, encouraging me to go clubbing with him, but it held no interest for me anymore. I didn't understand my feelings, why the death had affected me so much, but it had. My sister and Rory tried perking me up with progress reports on their baby's arrival, but I still felt depressed. My parents even attempted to cheer me, all to no avail. I knew I had to snap out of it, but I just couldn't. Not yet. Life had lost its flavor. Its vibrant color had faded, bleached by the tragic news. I confined myself to my residence, moping, unkempt.

"Incoming call from Jason," the audio-visual communicator announced.

I groaned. I knew what Jason wanted and why he'd called. Jason was a good friend. "Accept with visual."

"Hi, Ossy. How're things?"

I frowned. "Yeah, you know. OK, I guess."

"Let's go clubbing, buddy. No pressure. Just enjoy a few drinks. What do you think?"

I stared at Jason and saw the concern in his eyes. I knew I had to shake off my depression and move on, but I found it so difficult. Somehow, glimpsing the possibility of a relationship with Rebecca and then having it taken away so cruelly had exposed how empty my life was. But I knew Jason wouldn't give up. Resigned, I said, "Yeah, OK. I'll get ready and let you know."

Jason smiled. "Great. Same club around eight?"

I nodded.

We disconnected, and I stood wondering why I'd agreed. The weariness pressed on me as if I were in a high gravity well. I showered, shaved, and dressed, picking at a snack afterward. After flicking on my display, I saw a mountain of work orders demanding my attention, but I was going to forget that tonight, determined to just enjoy Jason's company if I could.

I waited, bored, but eight finally arrived, and I sat in my PR chair and dialed the venue.

———

People were lining up at the club's entrance. *Must be something special on.* I stood in line, edging forward at a snail's pace. The enthusiasm of the crowd rubbed off on me, and my gloom lifted a little. *I might even be alright as company.* I didn't see Jason. So, assuming he was inside the club, I patiently waited my turn.

With a sigh of relief, I crossed the threshold into the noisy interior. People shouted at each other, the blaring music colliding with their words. A throng cavorted on the dance floor, reminding me of Rebecca. I let the thought slip, determined not to burden Jason. After scanning the club and still not finding him, I strolled to the bar, thinking he might be there. He wasn't, so I ordered myself a beer while I waited.

A hand slapped my shoulder as I faced the bar. "There you are. Been looking everywhere for you."

I turned, grinning, to face him. "Hi, Jason. Want a drink?"

"Sure. I'll have a beer."

"Looks busy. Something special on tonight?"

"Not sure."

Jason hazarded an occasional nervous glance at me, as if wanting to raise a difficult topic but not knowing how, so I helped him. "I'm fine.

I'm determined to enjoy myself."

Jason smiled with obvious relief; the awkwardness was out of the way. "Great. So, what d'you want to do?"

"Let's find a table and just watch what's happening."

"I can live with that."

We took our beers and found a suitable spot in the outer perimeter, a semi-circular lounge with an excellent view of our surroundings.

"You've changed," Jason broached. "More sober, more mature or something."

"Haven't been hanging out around you." I smiled with a teasing edge but thought he might be right. Rebecca's death had transformed my perspective and increased my understanding of the fragility of life.

"Ouch, that hurt." Jason returned the smile.

"What happened makes you consider what's important."

"Yeah. Made me think too. Even I might have matured."

I chuckled. "Yeah. Maybe you have. I appreciate what you're doing for me with the calls and stuff."

"You're my friend. That's what friends do, right?"

"Well, I appreciate it." I gazed into my half-empty glass as I rotated it, not noticing two women approach our table.

"Mind if we join you?" one of them asked. I raised my head. Jason stared at me, alarmed. "Oh, sorry. Didn't realize you two were an item," the women added.

Jason panicked, which made me convulse with laughter. I patted Jason's arm.

"No, it's not that," Jason blurted. "It's just Ossy's had a shock, and I'm not sure if he's ready for company."

"His girlfriend dump him?" the other girl asked.

Jason became even more alarmed.

"It's OK," I told Jason as I slapped his arm again, giving him a sad smile. I looked at the women. "It's not that. My girlfriend died the other week, so I may not be in the best of moods." They both gasped at this. "But talking to you might be the medicine I need."

"You sure?" Jason asked.

"Yeah, why not? Won't hurt me."

The first woman who spoke was tall and thin, taller than me. She was dressed in a green sequined tee-shirt and tight black jeans. Her hair was short and black with a matching green streak, and she had an elongated face. The other was shorter, slimmer, with an elfin face like Rebecca's, I thought. Long blonde hair extended to below her shoulder blades, and she wore a skimpy red skirt with a white tank-top, just showing her cleavage. As I looked at them, I wondered which one would gravitate to me and which to Jason. I placed my bet and waited.

"I'm Jason. This is Ossy."

"Danny," the tall one said, pointing to herself, "and Tess."

"Have a seat then."

The women stood confused, unsure of their seating preference. Danny broke the deadlock and sat next to Jason. Tess stared at the spot beside Danny and then at the one alongside me. She looked at me and smiled. "Mind if I sit by you?"

"Sure." *I won my bet.* She came over and settled, keeping our personal space between us.

We talked for a time, the conversation light and non-threatening. It brightened my spirits as the night continued. I liked Tess. She was funny and easygoing.

"I'm sorry about your girlfriend," she said to me later on.

I glanced at her and saw sincerity and sadness in her eyes as if she had experienced a similar loss. "It was a tremendous shock. I've never heard of someone dying so young."

"Neither have I."

"Makes you appreciate life."

"Yeah."

We talked till after midnight, which surprised me. I didn't think I could stay sociable for that long, considering my continuing grief. We concluded the evening exchanging contacts and agreeing to call each other if we wanted to talk. I appreciated the gesture.

The night ended, and I returned to my physical world.

———

The monthly appointment to go outdoors arrived, and I prepared with less enthusiasm than usual. Still, I felt being in the parkland might calm my emotions. Two o'clock came, and the door unlocked, allowing me to leave my apartment for my outside time.

The wind was brisk as I stepped into the open, with cottonwool clouds racing across the sky. As I glanced up, it looked like rain threatened. I hoped not, as I had no protection against the weather and was reluctant to return inside to retrieve it. On continuing along the path and to my favorite seat, I sat and gazed out over the lake. The breeze whipped up the waves in the choppy water, making the occasional white head. Four ducks battled through the blustery conditions to gain access to a clump of reeds on the shoreline. They struggled but made it in the end and disappeared amongst the water grass. Large dark clouds gathered over the horizon, threatening to prove my misgivings right. *I'll just have to shelter under a tree if it rains.*

A small concrete ledge fringed the lake where it came nearest. Wanting a closer look at the water, I stood and walked over to it. The slab was smooth, with a film of slime covering it. I stepped onto it; too late, I knew that wasn't a good idea. I slipped on the slippery surface and fell, hearing a crack as I hit the ground hard on my left side. My wristwatch had slammed onto the solid surface, breaking it. *Great! How'll I know the time to return inside now?* Gingerly rising, I limped off the concrete ledge and returned to the seat, sulking over my damaged watch. My wrist hurt too, and I gave it a vigorous rub.

The light level dropped as the sun hid behind the clouds. I glanced up, observing the cloud cover extending over most of the sky. It reflected my darkening mood. I found little joy in life, apart from moments here and there. I kept track of how Cynthia and Rory were preparing for their child's approaching arrival, and Jason helped me escape my depression with his antics, but, apart from that, I just couldn't find much to give me purpose anymore.

Birds sang in the trees above me, and I closed my eyelids, listening to them. They sounded like sparrows, but I couldn't be sure. The music relaxed me as they spoke to each other with their song. There were slight differences between the birds' chirps. It felt peaceful ...

"Who are you?"

My eyes shot open. I glanced left and right and turned. A woman stood behind me. She held a small branch in her hand, ready to strike me, but she looked terrified.

"I ... I ... I ..." More words refused to escape. With a jump, I backed away from her, although she didn't look as if she intended to commit wanton violence. "I must have lost track of time."

The woman glared at me with suspicion. She was in her twenties and my height. Brown eyes and light-brown hair highlighted her freckled, heart-shaped face. She had a slender body and looked athletic. Her clothes included a maroon and green checkered shirt with blue jeans and navy sneakers. "That doesn't happen ... ever."

"You're right, but I fell. I broke my wristwatch, see." I showed her my shattered timepiece.

"Oh." The woman's tense stance relaxed, and she let the branch drop to her side.

I couldn't believe another person stood in front of me. A human in the flesh. "Are you real?"

"*Of course* I'm real. What kind of dumb question is that?" She glared, affronted.

With a downward glance, I blushed and said, "I mean ... it never happens ... I've never seen an actual person ... I mean not flesh-and-blood." I glanced back up and saw her frowning.

"Now that you mention it, neither have I." She scratched her head just above the right ear. "It never happens. We're released from our apartments once a month and we return at the end of our time slot."

"I'd better go. I'm eating into your time out here."

"You don't have to," she blurted.

"I'll get into trouble."

"Well, another few minutes won't matter if you're going to get into trouble, anyway."

"Suppose not ... I'm Oswald."

"Faye."

We both stood, half staring at each other and half trying not to stare, self-conscious that we had an *actual* person before us.

"What were you going to do?" I asked.

"What?"

"What did you intend to do today?"

"Oh, don't know. Walk along the lake, I expect. I do that most times. But I saw you, and you've confused me."

"Sorry."

Faye shrugged and grinned. "Well, at least you're something out of the ordinary. Not every day you meet another human in the flesh."

"No." I sniggered. "You want to walk together?"

Faye eyed me. "Yeah, OK." She dropped the branch and walked toward the lake. I took her lead and pulled up beside her as we strolled along the shoreline. We came to the concrete slab. "Don't step on that," I said. "That's where I slipped." Faye nodded, and we veered around it.

"You always here before me?" she asked.

"If you mean the hour before now, this day of the month, every month, yeah. Always have. And you?"

"Yeah ... and yet we've never met."

"I'm always diligent in returning when my alarm goes off — it's never occurred to me not to be." For the first time, that struck me as strange. "I've never set eyes on the person before me, neither. And I've never heard anyone mention they've met someone when outside their rooms."

"Me neither. Everyone's so conscientious. I wonder why that is? I'm terrible at keeping appointments and leaving on time, but not with my outer. Must be something ingrained in us from birth."

I walked in silence, thinking about how things had turned out. I could feel Faye bringing interest back into my life. It felt strange that I should meet three women in quick succession: Rebecca, Tess, and now Faye. Each one different, but each interesting in her own way. Faye was abrupt, judging by her introduction, but she mellowed.

"What's on your mind?"

I looked at her. "Not much. I had a girlfriend, but she died."

"Died?"

"Yeah. I know it just doesn't happen to a person our age, but it did. It hit me hard, and ever since I've been trying to get my life back together." I smiled. "I didn't know her long, but I knew she was someone special." We walked in silence for a few steps. "I wanted solitude after that, but my friend Jason convinced me to go clubbing recently for a drink. Got talking to a girl called Tess, and it felt good to communicate again. And now I'm chatting with you. All of you are different but easy to talk to."

Faye huffed. "That's not what my friends say. They suggest I'm a pain in the ass."

I laughed. "Maybe I need to know you better." I peered at her, and she at me, but we both looked away again as though afraid of the intimacy. The breeze picked up, and enormous drops of rain started falling. I glanced up and saw dark clouds. The rain turned heavy. "Quick, find a tree." I spotted a large oak with plenty of foliage for protection. "Over there." I pointed, and we both ran.

We were wet and puffing when we reached the immense tree trunk. I bowed, both hands grasping my knees.

"Woo ..." Faye's hair was stuck to her head, and her face dripped water.

I glanced up at her, and she stared at me. We both laughed. "You look like a drowned rat," I said.

"Speak for yourself," Faye replied with a beaming grin.

We kept laughing as Faye leaned against the tree. I stared out into the continuing downpour. "It might last a while. How much time do you have left?"

Faye glanced at her wristwatch. "Twenty minutes."

Gazing toward the complex, I pointed and said, "The trees are thick through there. We can start walking back that way?"

Faye looked. "Yeah, OK."

We strolled, darting across gaps in the foliage on occasions to avoid the rain until we reached the point closest to the living quarters.

"I'd better go. Sorry to disturb your time out here," I said.

Faye peered at her wristwatch. "I should return, too. No, you didn't. It was fun ... and different."

I went to leave but stopped and turned to her. "Would you mind if I lingered behind next month?"

She studied me for a moment. "Sure. It's interesting. That's if you don't get into trouble."

I huffed. "Yeah. With my luck, I'll get my next one canceled as punishment."

"Well, I'll know what happened if I don't see you."

"Until we meet again then."

"Yeah."

I hurried to the building entrance. When I turned to find her, I spotted her running toward another part of the complex. *I should have asked her for her contact details.*

5

CONFUSION

I OPENED the door and entered my apartment, still drenched from the rainstorm. I couldn't fathom the fact I had just seen another human being in the flesh. It could have been a PR experience. I'd had similar outings in PR in the past, even being wet by rain — although I was dry when I exited PR — but this was different. I'd changed inside, and I couldn't work out why. All I could think was: *why are humans kept isolated?* There was no one to ask. I'd just accepted it as natural, and I had met no one else who considered it odd.

"You are one hour late," a voice on the communication screen announced.

After jumping in the air as if attacked by an assailant, I looked at it. An unfamiliar image looked back at me. It had short blond hair and round, lobed ears with a triangular face composed of brilliant blue eyes, an aquiline nose, and thin lips. It was hard to tell whether it was male or female, but I assumed male. "Who are you?"

"You are one hour late."

"I fell and broke my watch. I lost track of time." The face stared out at me as if it didn't believe me. "See." I held up the broken timepiece.

"I will accept your excuse. Did you meet anybody?"

Frustrated, I asked, "Who are you?"

"That is not your concern."

"It is my concern. I wish to know who has my contact details and hacked into my communication system to such a degree that they didn't ask me to receive the call."

The face grew impatient. "Did you see anyone?"

"No, now go," I lied, glaring at it.

The face stared for several seconds as I glared back, determined not to break the impasse. "Very well." The screen blanked.

What was that? Who was that man? Are there secret police keeping track of our movements? I'd never heard of any. There's no point when everyone's locked in their rooms except for the hour they're released for their outer. Rumors would've spread if there were. I went and showered and changed into dry clothes as I pondered what it meant. After logging a repair request, I sent my watch in for repair through the courier pickup system from our apartments, and it returned the next day, functioning again. My greatest concern was my inability to raise my experience with anyone. They wouldn't believe me for a start, and after the call, it might be dangerous. Whoever it was might be listening.

As the days wore on, I remained distracted by the ordeal and started questioning my existence. Why were babies kept from their parents and only experienced family life via PR? Wouldn't it be more efficient to have a family unit together in one place? Why create it in an artificial environment like PR? I knew it wasn't real. I programmed parts of it.

Tess called me up on Friday afternoon to suggest I go clubbing with her and Danny. I didn't want to, but I agreed because I wanted to leave my apartment, even if it was only in PR. I dressed in casual clothes but made no genuine effort. Once I sat in the PR chair, I dialed the location.

———

The front of the club had no one waiting to enter. *It must be a quiet night.* I walked inside and scanned the place. It was definitely a quiet night. Few people congregated there. The music wafted at a low volume, accentuating the modest numbers, not thumping away in a claustrophobic crowd. *It might liven up later*, I thought. I checked for Tess, but she hadn't arrived yet. I ordered a beer at the bar. As I stared into the amber liquid, I wondered if it was real or an artificial reality simulation too. What was the purpose?

"Hi."

I looked around to see Tess standing behind me. "Hi. Want a drink?"

"Yes, thanks. I'll have a whiskey."

I ordered the drink. "Where's Danny?"

"She'll be here in a minute. She just had to get something. That's what she said. Goodness knows what the real reason is. Want to sit somewhere?"

"Yeah, sure."

Tess received her whiskey, and we walked to a table with a lounge nearby. "Thought you'd bring your friend."

"Huh? Oh, didn't think. I had things on my mind. He'll call if he wants to catch up with me."

"What's on your mind?"

I looked at her, wondering if I should mention my outside experience to her. *Would she believe me? She might tell someone and get me into strife. Is that mysterious man listening?*

"Just problems with my work. Nothing exciting. You know how it depresses you sometimes. Something crops up that irks you, and it sticks in your head."

Tess looked at me as if she knew I wasn't telling her the truth, but she didn't push the issue. "Yeah. That's annoying when it happens."

We sat in silence for a while, an impenetrable barrier strengthening between us. She didn't deserve that. She was decent, and I liked her, and she deserved to be entertained. I needed to snap out of my morose mood.

"You want to be somewhere else, don't you?" Tess said.

"No ... that's not it. I just find it hard to start a conversation sometimes." I peered out at the dance floor. Six couples cavorted on it in rhythm with the music. "You dance?"

Tess raised a brow in surprise. "Didn't think you danced."

"I don't," I said with a sheepish grin. "But it might help me snap out of the mood I'm in — if you dance, that is."

"Yeah, why not?"

We rose and joined the others, swaying to the tune's beat as we faced each other. I remembered Rebecca and how she just drew me to sway in synchronicity with her as if she had me on puppet strings. Tess wasn't talented in that way, but I saw she had experience. Within half an hour, we'd progressed from struggling to harmonize to coordinating our steps. Then we stopped and returned to our table. The club had filled with patrons in the meantime, although the attendance was still light for a Friday.

Tess glanced around the room. "Still no Danny."

"She didn't consider three a crowd?"

"Danny? No. Wouldn't have worried her."

I looked around and noticed Mandy walking near the bar. I wondered how she was coping with Rebecca's death and contemplated calling her over, but it felt rude. She looked around the place and saw me, giving me a weak smile. I could tell she still grieved. Seeing me may have brought back sad memories. I couldn't blame her, although I didn't know how close she had been to Rebecca. She came over after getting a drink. "How you doing?"

I sat confused for a moment, then said to Tess, "Tess, meet Mandy, Rebecca's friend." I turned to Mandy and shrugged. "Coming to terms with things."

Tess nodded.

Mandy's lips quivered, and she started to cry. "I can't get over it," she blurted, unable to control her tears.

"Come and sit," Tess soothed.

Mandy sat next to me and sobbed louder as she placed her drink on the table and put her head on my shoulder. I stared at Tess, at a loss.

"How could it happen? No one dies that young," Mandy got out between sobs.

I placed my arms around her to comfort her. "I miss her too, despite the brief relationship."

Gazing up at me, mascara streaking her face, Mandy whispered, "She said you might be the one. She couldn't stop talking about you."

I stared at her in shock. We had connected, but I didn't realize how much I had meant to her. The realization left me speechless.

Mandy glanced over at Tess, who sat in silence observing us. She let me go and wiped her tears away. "I'm sorry. I'm being rude. You're on a date, and I've butted in with my problems. Hope you don't think I'm trying to take him from you."

"That's fine," Tess said diplomatically. "And we're not on a date."

"I'd better leave, anyway. Good to see you again, Ossy."

"Yeah. Look after yourself."

After picking up her drink, Mandy stood and left.

I glanced at Tess. "That was uncomfortable."

"She needed to unload."

I nodded.

Mandy's presence had driven me back into misery again. Her revelation bewildered me. Knowing that Rebecca had thought that of me made it even more difficult to accept her death. I'd never gaze at her shining eyes and smiling face again. I sighed. "Not much company for you."

Tess touched my arm. "We don't need to talk to enjoy ourselves."

I looked at her with a wan smile. "No, maybe we don't."

A slower song started. "Wanna dance?" Tess asked.

Listening to the music's tempo, I wasn't sure. It meant dancing close, and I didn't know what would happen. Then again, we needed something to distract me, and Tess wanted it, so I nodded, and we strolled onto the dance floor. Tess put her arms around my neck and stared into my eyes. I placed my arms on her hips, and we swayed in rhythm to the music. After a while, Tess moved closer and placed her head on my shoulder, and I wrapped my arms around her waist. The intimacy made me reminisce about that other time with Rebecca, but I appreciated the warmth of Tess's body against mine, the intimacy of human contact, even though it was just PR contact. It comforted me but still didn't solve the confusion I had. We danced for several songs until Tess broke away to gaze at me again. She had sad eyes. I wiped my forefinger across her cheek. "What's wrong?"

"There's too much sadness. It feels empty sometimes."

"Well, if it's any consolation, you helped lift mine tonight."

She smiled. "You're welcome."

We returned to the table, and I said, "I want to go."

"Yeah, me too."

"Thanks for inviting me and for the company. I hope we can be friends and hang out again."

"We are friends," she said.

6

TOUCH

THE MONTH ELAPSED, and it was soon time to prepare for my next outer. I was excited both by the outing and the prospect of meeting Faye again. Thinking of her gave me shivers and butterflies. It was a strange sensation, as if I were dating, which was ridiculous. *I doubt she's even interested in me. I'm sure I'm not her type.* Still, I dressed in my good jeans and best tee-shirt. I then donned a black leather jacket because the forecast predicted cool weather, and I knew I looked good in it. I considered taking Faye a gift but then shook my head, alarmed at where my thoughts were taking me. Even so, something drew me to my work desk, and I pulled the top drawer open. A green miniature button shaped like a 4-leaf clover sat there, amongst my other collected junk. I picked it up and twirled it around in my fingers before pocketing it. I remembered receiving it when I was younger as a small give-away. It was my treasure then. I'll consider giving it to her.

The door unlocked, and I set off for my rendezvous, feeling more alive than I'd felt in weeks. A brisk breeze blew as I wandered to the lake. I veered left and strolled a different route than I usually took as I contemplated meeting Faye and what we might do. It had been ages since I'd traveled the trail, so I was keen to see if anything had changed. The forest ended, and open fields appeared with undulating green hills. As I gazed toward the horizon, a silvery structure flashed in the sunlight in the distance, looking for all the world like a large building on the shoreline. *But it couldn't be, could it?* I certainly couldn't recollect seeing it last time, but it may have been overcast.

My curiosity sated, I realized the hour was due to lapse and Faye would arrive soon. I strode toward the lake, not wanting to waste a second of our time together. As I walked, I considered what excuse I would give the strange man on my return indoors, if he appeared again, and what punishment he might inflict if my answer didn't satisfy him. I told myself I didn't care and would suffer the consequences.

Daffodils grew by the path, swaying in the breeze, just before the tree line. I picked two hoping Faye liked daffodils and continued my journey. My watch chimed as the seat came into view, but I barely heard it. All my senses were concentrated on searching for Faye. I neared the bench and spied her approaching. My heart leaped as she moved closer. She had dressed in a flamboyant blue top and jeans, had her hair in a ponytail, which flattered her face, and wore makeup. Perhaps she thought she was going on a date too. That thought made my heart race even faster.

"Hi," I said, trying to sound cool.

"Hi."

"Spotted flowers as I was walking, so I picked a couple for you. I hope you like them." I blushed and felt awkward and nervous as I handed them to her.

She gazed at the blooms and smelled them. "Who doesn't like daffodils? They're lovely. Thank you. No one punished you last time then?"

"No, but a strange thing happened when I returned to my apartment. A person called me and quizzed me about why I was late. I told him my watch broke, and he believed me. He asked if I'd seen anyone, but I lied and said I hadn't. I didn't want to get you into trouble."

"So, what's your excuse this time?"

I shrugged. "I don't care, except I'll be disappointed if I lose my outer."

She glanced at me, shy, and then looked away. "It'd disappoint me too."

Not knowing what else to do, I asked, "Shall I show you the fish by the jetty?"

"Please. I've never gone on the jetty before today. Don't ask me why, but I haven't."

We walked together, and I led her to the end of the pier. I looked over and spotted fish darting around near a pile. "Come look. There's fish here."

Faye crept to the edge, cautious, and peered into the water. "I see them."

As I gazed at her, I marveled at the animated expressions that flitted across her face as she observed the fish with delight — and, yes, I admit I also marveled at her athletic figure. I gulped and looked away before she caught me staring at her.

"That's so fascinating," Faye said, excited. "I've never seen real fish before."

We left the jetty in silence.

"Can I ask you something?" I ventured.

Faye gazed at me with a slightly apprehensive expression. It seemed every thought she had registered on her face. "Sure."

"Can I touch you?"

Her eyebrows rose. "Why?"

I stared at the ground and back at her, my expression earnest. "I'm wondering if it's the same as in PR. Just touch your hand."

"Yeah ... sure." Faye looked hesitant, but she extended her hand toward me.

I gazed at it. It was smaller than mine, with long, slender fingers and short fingernails. I reached out with my hand and touched her middle finger with mine. A shiver rushed up my arm as her smooth fingertip sent currents of warmth through me. I continued my experiment, bringing my other fingers to hers and looked up at her. She stared at our hands, fascinated. And, as she pushed her hand, her palm rose to face me. I copied her, and both our palms met, so soft and warm. I slipped my fingers between hers to complete my exploration and folded them over, staring at the two hands clasping each other. "It's like PR ... but different." I looked up at her.

She stared at our hands, mesmerized. "Yeah. More ... intimate ... physical ..."

"Real."

As if on cue, we stepped together and raised our other hands, grabbing them too, exploring each other's eyes. My heart thundered with anxiety and excitement. We moved again, our faces inches apart as we stood transfixed. To bring the scene to its climax, I closed the gap and kissed her. The sensual softness and warmth of her lips sent sparks of passion and exhilaration throughout my body. I broke off and backed away, gasping.

"That was ..." I began saying but couldn't finish.

"... sensational ... earth-shattering," Faye finished for me as she stared back at me, shivering.

"Did I shock you?"

Faye shook her head. "I'm overwhelmed."

"So, you agree you've never experienced this in PR?"

"Never ... and I've had plenty of kisses before this one. This was so ... personal. I can't put a word to it. What did you say? Real."

I nodded and then frowned. "Why do we interact only with PR? Why incarcerate us? We're prisoners. It makes no sense. Who is making us do this?" We parted.

"How can we ever find out?"

I grinned. "Maybe I'll ask the man if he shows up afterward. You want to go sit?"

Faye nodded, and we returned to the bench. By instinct, we held hands again. I couldn't forget the sensation. My thumb caressed the back of her hand in a subconscious movement.

I gazed out over the lake and watched the waves sparkle in the sun. "I must understand why we live as we do."

Faye looked at me. "How?"

"I don't know. Don't you want to know? Can you live your life as before, knowing the feel of real human flesh? I don't and can't. I'll go mad."

"But what can we do? We can't live out here. How'd we survive?"

I pondered her words. "Why can't we? Why can't we survive? It'd be tough at the start, but we'd acclimatize. And besides, we won't just live here. I need to meet whoever's doing this and ask why. We get food, drinks, clothing, and everything else delivered to us when we order it over the console. It has to come from somewhere."

"That sounds scary." Faye looked worried.

"We're smart people. We can research forest survival skills before we leave. There must be something somewhere about survival skills. People can't have lived cooped in rooms forever. They must have lived outside in the past." *Why had I never been curious about this before?*

"And we can pack what we can carry — to tide us over till we learn how to get food for ourselves," Faye answered, catching my excitement. "Energy bars don't take up much room."

She lapsed into silence, and I did, too.

"Where do we search for this mysterious force controlling our lives?" she said, breaking the silence.

"I don't know. I spotted a building in the distance while I waited. We could hike there and investigate it."

"What about our family and friends? What do we tell them?"

I realized she had an excellent point. We couldn't tell them we were leaving the complex, possibly for good. Cynthia and her baby came to mind. I might never see them if I fulfilled my intentions. I'd miss my friends, too, especially Jason. Would we be barred from our apartments if we left for an extended period? I sighed. "I don't know. But I have to do this. I'll understand if you don't want to go. It's your choice. You can contact me and tell me if you won't come. You can check if I've returned too."

There was a moment's silence before Faye answered. "I'm not sure if I could bear not seeing you again ... never touching you."

I had nothing further to say. Instead, I moved over and kissed her again. She pressed against me when our lips touched, and both our passions soared. I felt giddy as my head exploded and my heart raced. We parted, and I stared into her eyes. I wondered what she was thinking. What did she think of me? What if she ended up hating me once the novelty evaporated? Faye's chime sounded, and I looked at her watch, wishing I could rewind the hour.

"How good's your memory?"

"Reasonable. Why?"

"You'll have to remember my contact code." I told it to her and got her to recite it back several times. Satisfied she had memorized it, I rose and pulled the 4-leaf clover button from my pocket, giving it to her. "To remind you of me. Call me later, and I'll tell you what happened when I returned to my apartment."

Faye stood, too. She grabbed my arm and drew me to her again, kissing me one last time.

"We'll meet here next time, packed. Deal?" I asked.

"Deal."

7

DETENTION

EXPECTING the strange face to appear on my screen as soon as I walked in, I frowned when it didn't appear. I got a drink and visited the bathroom, then returned to the living room.

"Where have you been?" The face stared at me from the console. The voice was flat, unemotional.

"Outdoors."

"You're late in returning. You have a new watch. Where were you for the extra time?"

"Who are you?" *How does he know I've been outside for another hour? There's no surveillance out there that I've ever seen.*

"That is not important. You need to answer my question."

This person, whatever he was, was getting me agitated with his refusal to respond to any of my questions. "Why can't you tell me who you are? I've never seen you before, and you expect me to just give you anything you want to know. You're prying into my private life."

The face remained expressionless. "I'm your guardian. Answer me."

I glared in anger. "I don't need a guardian. Why are we locked up as if we're prisoners?"

"Where were you for the extra hour?"

"You answer my question, and I'll answer yours."

The man stared at me in silence until he said, "You are not captives."

"Then why are we restricted outside for only an hour a month? Why can't we go outdoors any time we want?"

"You need to answer my question."

He had me there. I seethed at it. "I was enjoying the fresh air, OK? And I wanted the extra time. Your turn."

"It is for your own good."

"It's not good for me. Don't I get a choice?"

"No."

"So, I'm a prisoner. As is everyone else."

"You are not prisoners. It is for your own safety."

"What do we need to be kept safe from? Where are you? Why hide from me? Where can I find you to talk to you in person? And I don't mean in PR."

"That is not possible. I will deduct the time from your next outing."

"That means I have to wait two months," I shouted.

"You should weigh your choices more carefully." The screen blanked.

I wanted to throw something, but there wasn't any unbreakable object within reach. Instead, I glared at the screen, my chest heaving in anger. *Two fucking months.* I sat and leaned back, closing my eyes to calm myself. *How can I wait two months to touch those lips again? Even a month?* I moved to the door and tried opening it, but it held fast, so I parked myself on the chair again, wallowing in my misery. What was the crime in being outdoors? At least he didn't mention Faye. The thought of Faye saddened me anew. Her face materialized in my mind, making me smile. I'd have to be satisfied with my memory for two months — unless she called.

As I opened my console, I scrolled through the news feed, having no energy to pursue any useful activities.

"You have an incoming call from an anonymous caller."

I gazed at the screen, my heart beating faster. The only unknown person coming to mind was Faye. She wasn't in my directory. "Connect with visual." Faye's face appeared and with it, my mood improved. She smiled but looked worried.

"Hi," I said. "You remembered."

"Yeah. You get a visitor?"

"Yeah." My face dropped, glum. "Not the greatest of conversations."

"Oh? So ... things still on schedule?"

I shook my head. "No. Got one taken away."

"Oh ... That's not fair." Faye frowned, looking frustrated.

"I can't do anything." I shrugged. "You can't reason with him."

"What're we going to do?" She looked sad.

"We can talk to each other. Go clubbing?"

"Yeah." She pouted and sighed. "Not much of a clubbing person."

"We can consider other things."

"What's your schedule?" She stared at me with a brave face and the hint of a smile.

"I'm not that busy. Jason calls to hang out sometimes. That's it unless I visit my sister."

"Who's Jason?"

"He's my friend from way back. I'm sure I mentioned him to you. Not sure if you'd warm to him. He can be obnoxious. A practical joker. Gotten me into tight spots more than once."

"Oh, that's right. He consoled you with Rebecca. What's with your sister?"

"She's married. They're getting their first baby soon. I might even get to see it."

Faye smiled. "Well, just thought I'd check how you were doing."

"I'm glad you called."

"Yeah, we'll work something out." Faye disconnected.

I sat back and smiled. My heart still bounced fast. *How will I last two months?*

I spent the time over the next week in drudgery. Nothing excited me, as the never-approaching day to meet Faye loomed too distant in the future. Faye called again, and we organized to dine at a restaurant on our rest day. Jason kept at me until I agreed to go clubbing with him on the Friday night. When I contacted Tess, she was busy, so it was just Jason and me. Despite my mood, I determined to make the most of it, conscious that if all went well, I might not be seeing Jason for a while, perhaps ever. I considered telling him what I was going to do but caution stopped me. He might try to dissuade me or might even insist on coming with me. The former I feared — he could be very persuasive — and the latter might complicate matters.

I didn't bother dressing up when Friday night came. Jason entertained me throughout the night with his amusing antics to get a woman's attention. He grinned with success by the night's end, but I drank too much.

———

My head throbbed the following morning as I woke. It seemed weird the PR chair duplicated our activities, including making us drunk in actuality. I should have known better since I was meeting Faye for lunch. I didn't need a fuzzy mind and a splitting headache. As I came to terms with my misbehavior, I rose and prepared to meet Faye. It would be the first time we'd engaged on PR, and I wondered how the experience would compare to meeting her for real. I'd find out soon. The rendezvous time came, and I sat in the PR chair, anxious and excited.

———

I scanned the restaurant as I walked in, nervous, but couldn't see Faye.

"May I help you, sir?" a server asked.

"Um ... I'm meeting a friend here for lunch, but she hasn't arrived yet."

"Did you reserve a table?"

"No."

"Oh ... a table for two is available." He looked at me and I nodded. "Over there." He pointed. "Would you prefer to wait for her at the table?"

"Yeah." He led me to it, and I ordered a beer and a carafe of water. I poured and gulped a glass of cool water when it came and then sipped my beer as I waited. I was starting to think she had stood me up when she walked into the restaurant. My heart pounded when I spotted her. She wore a low-cut red halter top with white jeans and white street shoes to match. She searched the room as I waved at her. When she recognized me, she smiled and strolled over to me.

"Sorry I'm late. Got held up getting here." She looked at me, confused.

I shared her confusion. I wanted to stand and kiss her but feared she might misunderstand. Bracing myself, I gave her a peck on the cheek. She blushed, and we both sat. I felt the discrepancy between this experience and reality straight away, and I saw she shared my disappointment.

"I have a hangover, so don't yell at me."

Faye frowned, then smiled. "What did you do last night?"

"Jason wanted to go clubbing, so I joined him." Faye looked hurt and unsure. "Oh, I wasn't trying to meet anyone. Jason obsessed over finding someone, though. He picked up a date in the end. I just got drunk. Stupid."

The explanation placated Faye. "You might control yourself next time."

I gazed at Faye. "Maybe there won't be a next time. Let's order our meals. It'll settle my stomach." We ordered our lunches and drinks.

Faye gave me a thoughtful glance. "Is it safe to talk about ... you know what?"

"Not sure," I said with a shrug. "I suspect he's got ears everywhere in here. Why wouldn't he? I think he created this, whatever this reality is."

Faye frowned. "How is that possible? Surely other humans built it, and humans must manage it."

"How come we've never seen them? Why is everything set up to isolate everyone?"

Our meals came, and we continued to talk while we ate. Faye peered at me. "How is your research going?"

I frowned but then smiled. "Just starting. There's so much to find out."

"So I've noticed. We have a cozy life."

"But unreal. Any second thoughts?"

She shook her head. "It's daunting, though."

I looked at her. I didn't want her to feel obliged to go with me, although I couldn't picture myself taking the leap without her, either. What we intended to do was frightening and crazy, and it put a small knot in my stomach when I considered it. But I had to do it. I couldn't live my isolated existence any longer, not after experiencing reality. I stared at the table. "Yeah, I agree."

We finished our meal and left. A park lay across the walkway from the restaurant. The garden had manicured lawns and wandering paths throughout. Flower beds decorated it too. "Shall we walk in the gardens?"

Faye glanced at it and back at me. She smiled. "Yeah, OK."

We strolled across the pathway. I ventured to hold Faye's hand as we walked. At first, she stared at our clasped hands and frowned, but then smiled. I smiled too when she accepted the gesture. We stopped to look at the flowers, Faye pointing at them and naming them with enthusiasm. I looked at her in wonder and hoped her knowledge extended to edible plants. "Where do you source your plant knowledge?"

"I studied them in school, and I've continued to study them since. In the past, I often visited places where different ones grew and observed them over a period, from when they spouted from the ground to when they flower and shed their seeds. Some then die, but others continue growing for the following year. I've had an interest in botany my whole life. It's beautiful."

"It makes you happy, doesn't it?"

Faye nodded and smiled. She let go of my hand and moved in closer, putting her arm around my waist. In response, I put mine around her shoulders. Her body warmed me, and I wondered in amazement, for the first time in my life, at the intricate detail of the PR's simulated reality. Still, now knowing the real thing, I detected the discrepancy. I held a minor role in that with my programming responsibilities, but someone or something must orchestrate it. Was it the man on the screen, or was another being controlling our lives? I frowned. Were these thoughts my thoughts or the thoughts of my artificial being? I remembered everything when I left PR, so they must be mine. Could the man read minds? I hoped not. Life would become intolerable if he could. Could he change someone's thoughts? I didn't think so. He'd remove my escape plan otherwise.

We spent two hours in the park, walking and discussing many topics. By the time we parted, I felt I knew her much better. She had two brothers and a sister, which was unusual. I only knew people who had just the one child allocated to them. We both promised to get together again soon, before returning to the lonely reality of our apartments.

8

ESCAPE

THE TWO MONTHS' detention had expired, and my next outing had arrived at last. All going well, I would not be coming back to my apartment at the end of my allotted hour.

I stared at myself in the mirror, my stomach tight and stressed. The image looked worried but determined. Would Faye have second thoughts? She had said she didn't, but it's different when you're crossing the threshold of no return. Our lives would depend on our own wit and ingenuity after this. We'd no longer have the comfort and trimmings of our present existence. Portable phones and other gadgets had no use outside our building. We both took data tablets filled with information and I developed a solar recharger for them based on plans I'd obtained from the WNN.

I felt guilty about leaving Jason without notice, but my biggest regret was leaving Cynthia and Rory. I had visited their PR place a week ago to see their new baby, a boy they were yet to name, and he was so tiny and cute. They were both so proud and protective of him, even though it all occurred in PR and the carer-bot did everything for the baby physically. It saddened me to think that I was forsaking seeing him grow up. I wouldn't even find out his name. But I knew they'd never understand why I was doing this. It'd horrify them. At least I thought it would — who really knew, given that we hadn't discussed it? But I couldn't run the risk of them trying to dissuade me. I comforted myself with the thought that I might return one day. I would miss Tess too, although I hadn't seen much of her since meeting Faye.

The door unlocked, and I stared at the last barrier, the tightness in my stomach increasing. I lifted my backpack and another duffle bag with clothing and essential items needed for survival outside. With a deep breath, I opened the door, stepped out, and, moments later, was in the open air. The day was sunny and warm, reflecting the norm for late spring. Birds sang in the nearby trees, but I couldn't identify them. As I lugged my bags, I struggled to the usual bench seat to wait for Faye.

———

I gazed across the lake. Two black swans launched from the surface and rose high before they disappeared past the tree line. Their rise to freedom mirrored the emotion I felt as I contemplated my decision. Artificial boundaries didn't limit them. But then I remembered the deer killed by the cat and realized that they too lived in constant danger. *What perils lay ahead of us?*

"Hi."

"Oh, hi," I said to Faye as I turned. "I didn't hear you come. I was miles away."

She smiled, but her face tensed with furrows across her brow as she stood with a backpack and duffle bag, too.

I rose but couldn't decide my next step. I wanted to touch her but didn't know her desires. She looked similarly uncertain, given her stance, eyes wide and body tense with indecision. Giving in to my need to approach her, I closed the distance and hugged her, gazed into her eyes, and kissed her. My world swam as the sensation hit me, and my heart raced. I broke the kiss and took in her presence again. "At last," I said between deep breaths.

Faye beamed a generous smile of joy, the brilliant whiteness of her teeth sparkling in the sunlight. She deposited her bags on the ground, and we both sat. "Well, this is it then."

"Yeah, this is it." I glanced over, wondering whether she was having second thoughts. "Not too late to change your mind."

"No, I want to do this. I'm just terrified."

I chuckled. "Me too. But if I return to my apartment now, that man'll lock me away forever."

Faye laughed. "Yeah. You just can't behave."

We both sat in silence, gazing at the lake, each in our own contemplations. I felt trapped in time, wanting to move, but frozen to the bench. With a sigh, I built my nerve and looked at Faye. "Shall we?"

She glanced back at me. "Let's, but where will we go?"

"I was thinking of finding that building I saw."

"Isn't that across the water?"

"Yeah. We'll try walking around the shore. I'm sure it's a lake or bay. We'll have to forget it if it's on an island."

Faye stood. "Let's go then." She put her backpack on and picked up her bag, raising a brow at me afterward.

I smiled at her display of eagerness and rose too, collecting my bags. We both took a breath and started walking toward our destiny.

9

GOODBYE

FAYE and I left for the lake mid-afternoon, knowing we'd soon need shelter for the night. We found a suitable spot in a small depression on the coastline. I had purchased a two-person tent, along with a bedroll, in my preparations for our escape into reality. I had expected my purchases to be denied, since we would never need such equipment, but I'd received them, no questions asked. I went camping in PR a few years back and we stayed in a similar tent, so I had an idea what we needed. Faye had a sleeping bag, too. Faye helped me set up the camp, which proved to be easy to do. We got a ration of food from our packs and ate our evening meal before darkness fell.

After preparing for sleep, we sat by the tent and studied our surroundings as dusk filled the sky, turning to twilight and then darkness.

"Doesn't it look wonderful?" Faye asked as she looked up at the starry heavens, a waning moon still hanging above the western horizon. "I don't remember ever seeing it this vivid. Am I imagining the distinction?"

"I'm not sure. It's different. But I just can't put it into words how." I glanced over at Faye, wondering whether to broach my concern. "Have you given more thought to finding food out here?"

"There's been nothing we could eat yet. I was hoping we'd pass by forests and other places where fruits and berries grow, so we can pick them as we travel. I have supplies for a couple of weeks. What about you?"

"I'm the same. We need to develop a routine before we get desperate. I couldn't buy a bow, so I'll have to make one if we want meat. And a spear as well."

"Phew ... that's terrible. You're going to kill an animal?"

"You want to eat steak?"

Faye grunted in frustration. "Glad you volunteered. I don't think I could do it."

"Wait until I've done it. I might chicken out when it matters."

We lapsed into silence, and I contemplated how different it was for me to sit with someone instead of alone in my apartment. I had been living in two dimensions, and now, without warning, I existed in three. Everything had a whole new breadth and perspective. So why were we imprisoned in our apartments to experience our social interactions via PR? I needed that question answered by whoever or whatever I found — if this person or thing lived within reach. I hoped to find a clue inside the building. I glanced at Faye and saw her zoned out in her own world. "Any regrets?"

She turned to me and snorted. "It's only been a few hours. Ask me again when we're out of food and starving."

I smiled and nodded. "I think I'll go to bed."

"OK. I might too soon."

I went into the tent and slid into my bedroll. With the warm night, I let it stay open. I closed my eyes and attempted to drift into sleep. Faye's shuffling disturbed me later, but I didn't acknowledge her as she slipped into her sleeping bag. I fell asleep.

When I woke to the dim light of pre-dawn, Faye lay with her arm draped across my chest. I wanted to move but was reluctant to disturb her. Her warmth relaxed me, and her slow, steady breathing lulled my ears as she inhaled and exhaled through her half-open mouth. I wondered what she would think if she caught me looking at her in her sleep, and I smiled. She had no fear of my intentions toward her, which surprised and pleased me since we didn't know each other well. Unable to tolerate lying there any longer, I lifted Faye's arm with care and slipped out from under it, replacing it on the ground. She muttered but didn't wake.

After leaving the tent, I walked to the beach nearby and watched the waves lapping the shore as the sunlight increased in intensity. The salty air teased my nostrils. Flocks of birds cruised the water a hundred yards out to sea, drifting with the current. Now and then, one disappeared and re-emerged with a fish in its beak. The sun flared as its orb rose above the horizon and dappled the sea's expanse with sparkling light dancing across the swell. The moment's serenity gave me peace for the first time since Rebecca had died. Footsteps interrupted my reverie, and I turned to see Faye strolling up to me. "You're awake."

"I got cold."

"You were on top of me."

Faye's eyes widened.

"I ... mean ... you rolled up next to me and had your arm on me."

"Oh."

"I'm not complaining — it felt nice."

She smiled and looked toward the view. "It's beautiful."

"Yes. Peaceful."

"There's a large forest across the water." Faye pointed. "We might have luck with food if we can hike to it."

"We should have something to eat. Then pack and break camp."

We reluctantly left the beach and returned to our tent, dismantling it and packing it away with our sleeping bags. I opened my canteen and had a drink. As I rummaged through my bag, I found an energy bar and ate that. Faye snacked on one too and was then ready, so we started walking again, following the coastline.

The day warmed, both of us sweating. After stopping for a break at midday, we found a deep stream blocked our path ahead. We fretted on our next move, but with no other choice, we followed the waterway back toward its source, hoping to find a suitable crossing. A sparse wood came into view as we continued our trek, the ground undulating. I heard splashing water, and minutes later, a waterfall and a pool lay in our way. As I surveyed the landscape and saw that the cliff extended into the distance, I concluded we needed to detour inland to reach the top of the waterfalls. Late afternoon approached.

"We should camp here tonight," Faye said.

"OK. It's sheltered, and there's plenty of drinkable water. There could be food nearby."

"That sounds good. I'd enjoy a quick dip."

"Yeah. Might search for wood to light a fire. And spear or bow-making materials."

We dropped our bags and assembled the tent. I left looking for firewood. After lugging several bundles back, I set off again and searched for timber suitable for weapons, finally finding a branch to shape into a spear. With the serrated knife from my scabbard, I hacked the limb off and removed the leaves and smaller twigs. It felt heavy and balanced in my hand. I put it over my shoulder and headed back to camp. The sound of splashing made me stop as I broke through the tree line. Faye was frolicking naked in the pond. I averted my eyes, feeling awkward, not knowing whether to wait for her to finish or warn her that I'd returned. The sight of her body covered in a sheen of water gave me shivers. I withdrew and sat on a nearby rock and started paring the shaft end into a point. It looked reasonable after half an hour, so I returned to our campsite, relieved to see Faye sitting there, clothed.

She turned around when I approached. "Where have you been?"

"I found a branch and fashioned it into a spear." But I glanced downward. "I returned a while ago, but you were swimming in the water. I didn't want to embarrass you, so I left."

Faye blushed. "Oops. Hope you didn't see too much."

"Enough." I cracked into a sheepish grin. To break the pregnant silence, I said, "I'll get a campfire going."

"Did you notice any food on your travels?"

"No, but I wasn't paying attention."

"I might explore then."

"You won't get lost?" I had a panic attack that she would.

"I'll stay nearby."

"OK."

She left with a container, and I started a fire with wood shavings.

They burst into flames; the small twigs ignited next as I fed the camp-fire with them until the larger pieces of timber caught alight. It wasn't long before I had a decent fire going. The fire crackled as the residual moisture exploded from the burning logs. I set up a kettle kit from my duffle bag over the coals and filled the pot with lake water for both of us, intending to make coffee. The water boiled just as Faye returned from her expedition.

"Any luck?" I asked.

"I found berries — blackberries, I guess, judging by the scratches I got picking them."

"Coffee?"

Faye's eyes brightened. "Yes, please."

I made two coffees and handed her one. The aroma reminded me of the coffee I drank in the PR cafes, but the intensity of the fragrance was richer. Faye placed the container of fruit between us, and we ate them between sips, the berry juice staining our hands. The light began deteriorating once we finished. I yawned, and I saw Faye copy me moments later. She looked at me and giggled. Birds warbled as they prepared to settle for the night, and a cricket chirped once darkness fell.

"Walking makes you tired," I said. "I might go to sleep."

"OK."

I retired into the tent and settled into my sleeping bag. The remnants of the fire gave a dim glow through the canvas material as the embers exhausted themselves. As I lay on my back, I placed my hands behind my head, thinking through the day's events. We had achieved little in reaching our goal, but we'd gained valuable experience for our survival.

Faye came in, wriggled into her bag, and positioned herself next to me, rolling onto her side. She looked at me as I thought, so I turned to her. After lifting herself up and over me, she reached across and kissed me. I lifted an arm and draped it around her shoulders as the kiss became more intense, arousing me. I wasn't sure of her intentions and was too afraid to ask. We broke off, gasping. I stroked her hair, the silky strands sliding through my fingers. Her eyes sparkled in the scant light. I placed my other arm under her head, and she rested on it as she continued looking at me. As she raised her torso again, she unzipped her sleeping bag and fumbled for the zip on mine. After finding it, she opened it and shuffled over so we could lie together, our clothes the only barrier between us. We kissed again, and she slipped her hand under my shirt. My urge intensified. I cupped her breast. Overcome with an urgent need, we struggled in a flurried frenzy to unclothe. Our fever increased until we both heaved in ecstasy, and Faye nestled into me, our residual sweat intermingling on our bare skin. I had never experienced such intensity, not even with Rebecca. I fell asleep with her wrapped in my arms, her head on my chest.

Birds singing woke me the next morning. Faye still lay on me, naked and sleeping, her leg draped over me. Her warmth seeped through me and gave me a sense of fulfillment. But I wondered how long this idyllic existence could last. I recalled the night's events, and it occurred to me she needed the intimacy, the intensity of contact, to confirm she wasn't alone. After consideration, I realized I, too, hungered for intimacy. Maybe our heightened need had started the frenzy. Faye stirred and opened her eyes, looking at me with a sleepy smile. I bent my head, brushed my lips against hers, and let her roll off me.

"That was unexpected," I said.

"I needed you."

"I think I needed you too."

Faye giggled. "There goes my modesty."

I smiled. "I suppose so."

We both rose and left for the lake, bathing in the chilly water, romping together, and enjoying joining as one. We then dressed, had breakfast, and packed. I suggested we cross the river where it exited the pond, as the stream looked shallow there. We took our trousers off and waded through with our bags raised above our heads. The stream reached our hips, but we managed to get across and continued our trek.

10

THE BUILDING

WE RETURNED to the shoreline and continued our journey to the building. The coast curved around a bay until we reached the far shore by the evening. More vegetation covered the countryside on this side as well — large, luscious bushes, trees billowing their foliage, and flowers scattered along our way. I picked violet irises for Faye. She blushed as I gave them to her, and we laughed.

The odd bush had berries on them, and Faye said they were edible. We plucked them and ate our fill for the day. It was difficult for us to carry any, as we had no suitable containers, except for the lidless one Faye carried.

As dusk approached, we set up camp for the night, and I gathered wood for a fire. The shoreline where we stopped had a rocky edge, gray basalt facets plunging into the sea, a huge battlement to protect the land from the pounding waves. I tiptoed along the bank and gazed into a calm backwater, where it disappeared into the abyss. Several underwater shelves extended out from the sheer rock face, and fish swam leisurely into the open from underneath them. I rushed to fetch my spear and returned, studying the fish's movements as they wove their way through the gaps. After taking aim, I thrust the weapon into the water and, by a miracle, the point pierced the creature behind the gills.

With a yank, I raised the weapon. The fish flapped seawater over me as it ended its life. I took it to a grassy patch and gutted it as I'd seen it done on the central library's archive footage. I carried it back to the camp with a proud smile.

Faye glanced up when I returned. "Phew ... what's that?"

"A fish. I caught it. I'll cook it for our meal."

"We're going to eat that?" Her face looked disgusted.

"Yeah. You've eaten seafood before."

"Yeah ... but ..." Faye stared at the fish, then at me. She projected a lingering fear. "I didn't realize they came that way. Those eyes are creepy."

I laughed, turned around, and sat with the fish facing away from her. With a quick slice, I severed the head, leaving it hidden from sight. "That better?"

She stared at the headless carcass, still dubious until she gave a resigned shrug. "I suppose."

Walking over to the fire, I scraped together glowing embers to the side and set the fish on them to grill, flipping it with my knife a few times until it looked cooked, and I put it on a plate from my backpack to cool. I salivated as I waited, the aroma wafting toward me. I peeled the skin off the top with my blade and pulled out a large flake of flesh, sliding it into my mouth. The flavor of freshly caught and grilled fish exploded as the morsel touched my tongue, my eyes closing to savor the delight. I could not describe the sensation. "Eat." I smiled to encourage Faye.

She stared at the fish, wary, but took the chance and tore out a portion, tasting it. Her eyes widened. "Wow, that's delicious." She devoured it and ripped off more, gorging it as she licked her fingers in between bites.

"Hey, leave some for me," I said, grinning.

"First come, best dressed." She gave me a wicked smile.

I dove in and consumed my share as we sat, pulling out the center spine when we finished the top side. Little food remained after another ten minutes. Our stomachs sated, we ate a few berries and reclined, talking for the rest of the evening before retiring. After zipping our sleeping bags together to make one large bag, we both got in and cuddled as we fell asleep. It was one of the happiest days of my life, and I wanted to relish its memory as I dozed.

The next day started sunny, with a slight sea breeze. It warmed as we packed our belongings away and began hiking again. We hoped to get to the mysterious building before nightfall. As we crested a hill along the shoreline just after midday, the edifice came into view. It was silvery, but I couldn't judge how large it was from where we stood. We walked another two hours before we approached its perimeter.

Now, seeing it up close, I saw it was an enormous construction. It had no windows on the side we faced, but we hadn't examined the far end yet.

"What is it?" Faye asked. She looked as puzzled by the construction as I felt.

"I don't know. A strange place to put a building. There's no access to it."

Faye's eyes shot open in surprise. "Hear that?" The sound of operating machinery reverberated from the building's interior. The hum fluctuated as if motors loaded and unloaded again.

"Let's go check the other end."

We walked the short length, and what we saw surprised us. Two large doors provided access, but they were closed when we rounded the corner. A concrete road wound away from the spot. I could only imagine its destination. Trees lined the way on the landward side and extended into a sparse forest of oaks, although Faye noticed fruit trees grew further afield and said we should investigate them later.

As we couldn't gain access, we walked off to the first line of trees and sat facing the building's closed doors. *Why erect a building at this location?* It was near our accommodation complex but inaccessible across the bay. Another strategic asset must decide this position. I stood and searched to discover the reason. But just the forest and the sea surrounded us. Maybe it needed cooling water, but it could source that from anywhere in the bay. The land rose from our spot for half-a-mile inland, so what lay over the crest was invisible. "Let's go walk to the top of that rise. We might see something from there."

"OK," Faye said and stood.

We both strolled into the forest and up the hill. The view from the hilltop stunned us. A vast plain of neatly planted vegetables, lined with rows of fruit trees, extended into the distance.

"We don't need to worry about starving," Faye said.

I looked on in amazement. Why is this garden here? Where do they take the food? Someone had placed the trees and vegetables there. Nothing in nature aligned the plants with such a neat orientation. Who or what tended the plants? "Do you know what they are?" I asked Faye.

"Those look like corn. Let's investigate." We strolled the short distance to the garden, and Faye went to have a closer inspection. "Yeah, it's corn," she said as she slipped the leaves through her fingers.

I wandered over to different plants. They had fern-shaped fronds with an orange base. I leaned over to take one and saw it was a carrot. After brushing the dirt from it, I took a bite. The crisp, sweet carrot refreshed my mouth as I chewed. Its taste resembled the food we had in the complex but fresher. You couldn't get fresher than straight from the garden.

Faye came over to me. She pulled a carrot from the ground, too, and started chewing it after removing the dirt. "Look," she said as she pointed further away. "Lettuces and other plants still further out."

"How do they keep the wild animals from stealing the crop?" I wondered out loud.

Faye smirked. "You mean like us?"

I smiled at her. "Yeah. Why aren't more animals feasting on this food?"

An ominous sound pulsed from the distance, and we both looked toward it. A gigantic spider-looking machine was working its way toward us, following the line of the crops. It had large rubber tires that fit between the rows. There were twenty rows or more between the wheels on either side. I stared at it, fascinated to discover its purpose. A massive bulbous body with a cabin unit and a rotating turret scanning its surroundings sat on top. Without warning, a blue blast of laser light burst from the turret toward the ground a hundred feet from the machine. A puff of smoke rose from whatever it hit.

"I guess that answers your question about lack of animals," Faye said.

"We'd better hide before it gets here and decides we need exterminating," I said to her, worried it had spotted us and that was the reason it was coming our way. We both retreated into the tree line and hid behind a tree's massive trunk. The equipment worked its bulk to the vegetable garden edge and stopped. The turret rotated back and forth for several minutes before the vehicle reversed and receded, retracing its path. We noticed it removing random plants as the behemoth continued its lumbering way. We watched the machinery until it became a distant spot before stepping out from behind the tree.

"I want to gather more carrots. The corn isn't ready yet, but we could get lettuce," Faye said. We went back and pulled six carrots each, Faye wandering over to the lettuces and grabbed one. I scrutinized the direction where the machine came from in case it returned, but Faye walked further away and picked red bulbs from other plants before returning to me. "Capsicums," she said. "Let's check the fruit trees. They might have ripe fruit on them." Approaching them, we spotted red apples hanging in clusters ready to be harvested. I climbed up the tree trunk and plucked four apples off, tossing them to Faye below me.

"That will last us several days," I said, considering our collection. "Let's go back toward the building. I want another peek."

"You think that's wise? Those laser weapons might be somewhere."

"We won't know if we don't look." I led Faye back to the edifice, and we sheltered under a tree, observing the two doors again. "They must open some time."

"We need to pick a place to pitch our tent soon," Faye said after no action occurred from the building or anywhere else. "Let's get away from here. I'd prefer being out of sight in case there's surveillance."

I glanced over at her. She looked worried. "Yeah." I scrutinized the surroundings, and we retraced our tracks to gain distance from the doors and the access road for now. Once away from the construction, we set up camp, and I lit a fire.

Dusk started as the fire blazed and the chill of night descended on us. Faye shivered, so I put my arms around her to lend her my warmth. She leaned her head back on my shoulder and smiled at me before turning and kissing me. We sat, Faye fitting between my legs as I continued warming her. We ate two carrots each and tore lettuce leaves off, eating them too. I cut a capsicum in half and gave one piece to Faye while I had the rest. We both finished with an apple, the juice dribbling from my chin as I bit into the crisp flesh.

I tossed the apple core away, wiped my mouth clean with the back of my hand, and rested my head on Faye's shoulder. Her delicate strands of hair brushed against my cheek. Her scent excited me. Faye glanced around as she felt my desire for her, so we retired to the tent.

A noise woke me early the next morning, so I slipped from the sleeping bag, careful not to disturb Faye yet, and dressed. I headed toward the sound, which came from the building's direction. Daylight was banishing the night's darkness. I kept to the forest and angled around until I observed the two front doors. One stood open, and a vehicle lay idle half inside the doorway. It moved backward a few yards intermittently, and I realized that the sound of its movement had woken me. The building engulfed the whole thing half an hour later. After a few minutes more, it drove off along the road and disappeared. When I saw the whole vehicle, I realised it was a truck from videos I watched when I was younger. I didn't know whether it was full or had just deposited its load. No cabin existed. The door closed soon afterward. The truck's engine faded into the distance, leaving me with nothing more to see, so I returned to the camp.

"Where have you been?" Faye half-shouted at me when I came back. "I thought you'd deserted me or something." She looked distraught.

Chastised by her fear, I lowered my gaze. "I'm sorry. I went to investigate a noise. You were asleep, and I didn't want to wake you. It was early. A truck arrived at the building, and it was loading or unloading. But the walls obscured my view." I walked over to her and stroked her cheek.

Faye calmed, but I could tell she was still mad at me. "Wake me up next time. I don't appreciate being left alone, not knowing where you are."

"OK, I will. Sorry."

Placated, Faye nuzzled into me and wrapped her arms around my waist. I put mine over her shoulders and brushed her hair as she rested her head on me.

11

INSIDE

IN THE MORNING, we strolled to the beach and bathed, leaving our clothes on the sand above the high-tide mark. We dried off afterward in the sun as it rose higher, the rays warming our skins as we stood naked. Any shyness had vanished with the intimacy we now shared.

After dressing and eating, we returned to the building, hoping to gain more information. We didn't have long to wait. Another truck crested the hill along the road and stopped in front. A door opened, allowing it to enter.

I glanced at Faye. "I want to see inside the building."

"Should we?" Faye frowned.

"I don't know, but we won't learn what's there if we don't."

"I'm coming with you, then. At least if something occurs, it happens to both of us."

I was uncomfortable bringing Faye along, but she had a point in not separating. Besides, I doubted I could convince her to stay given her earlier reprimand. We both crept toward the factory and stood before it a few minutes later. I couldn't detect any surveillance on the outside, but whoever controlled this may have far more advanced technology than we had in our complex. As we held hands, we took a tentative glance beyond the corner at the truck, Faye sheltering behind me.

The vehicle stopped in the doorway. I looked back at her and nodded. We sneaked around the exterior and to the entrance. There was nothing to prevent our snooping, so we rounded the opening and entered. Huge drones hovered by the rear of the trailer, their spinning rotors humming away like gigantic mosquitoes. Four arms dangled from them with hooked ends, one drone holding a large crate with the hooks inserted in slots at the bottom. It flew off, replaced by three others waiting in line.

I scanned for any surveillance equipment but saw none, and no sentries patrolled inside the building. My pulse steadied with my fear of danger abating, and I straightened my stance, looking back at Faye with an air of confidence. One I didn't have.

"It's a storage depot," Faye whispered.

"We're only seeing the front end of it. We need to explore the rest of it." I took a step, but Faye's grip stopped me.

"The door might close while we're inside the place. How will we get out?"

I acknowledged her point. A closed door would trap us inside until the next truck came along unless we could find an alternative entry mechanism. How did the doors open when a truck delivery arrived? Did they communicate with the building communication network, or did they trip the opening controls on arrival? We could test the second means by waiting for the truck to leave and tracing the path it took to check if we could open it. It still left the problem of getting out — unless the door stayed ajar until a later activation occurred, making it close. With disappointing indecision, I looked at Faye and then into the bowels of the construction, craving to explore but knowing self-preservation needed to stay top of our priorities at present. "OK, we'll go outside, but I want to try something when the vehicle leaves." We slipped back around the corner and waited.

"What's inside those containers?" Faye asked. "There're lots of them."

"Don't know. They're sealed, and they have no markings on them, none that I can see. We won't find out until we investigate the rest of the building."

The truck took half an hour to unload, and when it left, the building's door closed behind it. We both walked along the pavement, following the vehicle to the crest. "The trucks followed a pre-determined path as they arrive. You follow those wheel marks, and I'll check the ones on this side," I told Faye as I pointed to the markings on the road. "We'll walk back to the building. Find out if we trip an opening mechanism."

We both strode to the entrance, careful to tread in the tire tracks. Nothing occurred until we were twenty yards from the entrance when the door started sliding open. I froze. Faye did the same. The sound of drones starting their rotor motors erupted, the bodies of the monsters coming into view moments later, their spidery frames hovering just inside the doorway, waiting for something to unload.

"What now?" Faye asked.

"Let's sneak forward until we reach the door and then retrace our path."

Faye nodded and made a mark where we stood, so we would know when we returned to the activation position again. Intrigued, we stepped toward the building, the noise of the drones growing louder. We reached the entrance, the craft still hovering, ready for duty, then turned and walked back. Nothing happened when we returned to the opening point.

I frowned and looked at Faye, wondering if we had scrambled the controls with our phantom delivery. "Let's go inside to where the truck stops when it's unloaded. The closing trip could be there."

"The door might close on us."

"I don't think so. The truck leaving activates the closure. There's a delay until it departs."

"If that's the case, we can get out whenever we wish."

We returned to the building and ventured inside it. The unloading machines hovering overhead remained stationary, to my relief. I didn't want a drone chasing me to deliver me to a stockpile for processing. We stopped when we arrived at the spot we thought the trucks reached when empty, turned, and walked out. The door closed as we left and we watched the drones move to their parking position before the shutter blocked our view.

After motioning to Faye to follow me, I went to the vegetable garden and sat. Faye rested beside me. I grabbed a twig and scribbled on the ground as I thought through our discovery. The door's opening-and-closing mechanism was decisive, the means of detection remaining unknown. After glancing at Faye, who squatted waiting, I said, "That's straightforward, but what if a truck comes while we're inside and closes the entrance before we leave?"

"I know I was frightened before, but it won't be a disaster. We can just wait for another truck to arrive. I presume they come at regular intervals." As if on cue, we heard a vehicle crest the hill, headed for the building, making Faye smile.

"Let's get a bag of food supplies and a jacket in case it gets chilly, or we're trapped overnight. Then we'll have a decent search."

Faye agreed, so we returned to our camp and packed energy bars and other items, arriving back at the warehouse as the truck left. We discussed what we should do and decided to wait for the next truck instead of tripping the door open ourselves. We sat on the ground nearby, using the time to fill each other in on the important events of our past life. Faye's varied and colorful history counterbalanced my more routine upbringing. She said, being the eldest child, she always got into trouble, even though it was one of the others who misbe-haved. Her parents said she should know better. She outlined the antics they did, which made me laugh. Knowing these things about her gave me an insight into her personality. I presumed it was the same for her.

The familiar noise of a truck arriving grew louder and one crested the hill, coming to a stop in position at the factory moments later. We stood and strode over, crossing the door's threshold. My heart thumped with anticipation and concern. The perimeter inside the building was devoid of any stacked containers — these only occupied the vast interior warehouse space — so we crept along the wall to the back, checking for an opening to the rest of the factory. One such orifice existed twenty feet in from the side. A conveyor pierced the barrier. We walked over to it and watched it move boxes from the store through the partition. I presumed a drone lifted the crates from their storage location and placed them on the belt, allowing the crate to transfer to the other side. A gap gave us access to slip past, so we sneaked through, searching for danger, but saw none. A large processing plant lay before us, the purpose of it a mystery at present.

"Look!" Faye pointed at a crate twenty feet away. "That one's open. Let's check inside it."

The conveyor ended ten feet ahead. We rounded it and crept to the box. Carrots came into view as we approached. The container stood on a platform that tilted into an adjacent bin. "This must be a vegetable-processing plant," I said, the machinery piquing my interest. There were six similar platforms on this end of the machinery, but they lay idle at present, with the equipment extending further into the building, access ways spaced between them. I walked to one of these, Faye close behind me, and gaped at the machines as they towered over us. We arrived at the rear of the factory. Dispatch tables with packaging machines and empty crates stood alongside the line, ready for filling.

A deafening noise reverberated through the place as the machinery started up, making me jump in fright. Faye reached out and grabbed my arm, causing me pain as her fingernails bit into my skin. We both stared as the machine's hum increased.

"We should leave," Faye suggested.

I thought it a good idea, so I turned to retreat.

"What's that?" Faye asked, fearful as she pointed upward.

A dangerous-shaped drone flew toward us. Its compact form had a long thin nozzle extending from the bottom with a turret mechanism that allowed the craft to aim the shaft. We found out its purpose moments later when it shot a blue laser, missing us and hitting the floor ten feet away. I grabbed Faye's hand and started running to the front of the factory, Faye screaming in fear as the drone turned and followed us with its menacing hum buzzing overhead. Two more blasts flashed by as we zigzagged up the access aisle.

I heard another shot zing past me. I thought it had missed me but a few moments later, I felt a throbbing in my upper arm. In between our circuitous run, I glanced at the pain's source. Blood welled from a wound.

We reached the front of the line and dashed for the gap in the wall by the conveyor belt, entering the warehouse. Thinking the danger was gone, I stopped on the other side to regain my breath; Faye did likewise. But the predator kept coming. Realizing our mistake in stopping, I shouted, "Run!"

The truck moved, leaving the factory as we restarted our dash, and the door began closing. The last thing we needed was to be trapped inside with a killer drone.

I pulled Faye along as she stumbled to keep up with me, with the assassin rising and continuing its hunt.

The exit was half-closed when we started running, the gap diminishing with every step we took.

Fear of not making it gripped me as I urged Faye to run faster.

The shutter continued its relentless travel.

The opening was three feet wide when we approached it, and Faye squeezed through just before the door shut, the angry drone buzzing at us as I glanced over my shoulder in relief.

12

SEARCHING

Faye and I stared at each other with sheer terror as we gasped for air. Our narrow escape had rattled me — not just my brush with death but knowing that Faye had almost suffered the same fate. I saw how shaken she was by the experience, and I blamed myself. I led her toward the surrounding forest.

"You're injured!" Faye whispered as she pointed to my arm.

As I glanced down, a trickle of blood oozed from a burned patch of my shirt, but it was already starting to dry. It intrigued me. It wasn't painful. I released Faye's hand and touched the hole, opening it to see the underlying flesh. A minute circle of raw meat, the size of a fingernail, exuding a limpid liquid. "It doesn't look serious."

"Does it hurt?"

I shook my head and forgot the injury, glancing back with disappointment and frustration at the building. We couldn't return inside for a closer inspection. We had alerted the drone to our presence. At least we now knew it was a food-processing factory. "If trucks bring carrots etcetera into the place, others must remove the product. I wonder where they go?"

"The rigs have enclosed trailers. We wouldn't know. They might travel to our living complex," Faye said.

"That's true. We could check the vehicles' movements and watch them loading or unloading. I'm sure the drone won't come out looking for us."

"I don't want to step anywhere near that building again. We need to move somewhere else."

"Where?" I stared at the factory, forlorn at the prospect of leaving with my questions unanswered, and then at the route the trucks had traveled to deposit their cargo. "We could follow the road. See where that leads us."

Faye looked at me with a frustrated glare. "To what end?"

"To discover whoever controls this. He must be somewhere."

"And what if he's not? What if we never find him?"

"Do you want to go back?"

Faye shook her head and frowned. "No, I just detest not knowing what we're doing."

I sympathized with her frustration and reached over to rub her shoulder. "I don't like it either, but we'll have to improvise until we spot a clue."

Faye looked at the ground, brooding, until her eyes latched onto my injury again. "Do you need something for that?"

"It's nothing."

"We should clean it and bandage it. I've got a first-aid kit in my bag."

Appreciating the attention, I allowed Faye to lead me to our camp, where she attended to my scratch. Still, I shivered when she wiped the dried blood away as I comprehended what could have happened. Her tender touch soothed me, and I smiled back at her when she looked up from her work on my arm. She had the skill of an experienced physician, a florist arranging flowers, or an artist placing the last pencil-thin stroke of paint onto the canvas. "Thanks," I said when she finished.

We sat beside each other, gazing at the sea lapping the shoreline, lost in our own thoughts. Mine drifted off to what options we had in our search for this mysterious deity looking after humanity, as that is what I called the landlord, overseer, manager, or whatever name he, she, or it had. The only suggestion I had was the one I mentioned to Faye — follow the road and hope it offers further clues. I looked over at her, wondering what she thought. The sun had risen to midday when I said, "We should leave."

Faye nodded. "I want to pick more fruit and vegetables before we go."

"We can do that." I stood. "We need to watch out for the guard drone." I wandered back to our camp and began packing things away. Faye followed moments later and did likewise. When we finished, we gazed at each other, nodded, and started walking, stopping at the field to collect vegetables and fruit. I acted as a lookout while she worked.

We adhered to the verge as the road wound its way along the coast. Trucks passed by us several times but ignored our presence. Hills and mountains soared to our left as we headed east. The hillsides were green with grass. As we walked, I pointed out to Faye the occasional white spot in the distance that appeared to move as time elapsed, wondering if it was a grazing animal. Large trees populated the sides of the mountain slopes, a few peaks with snow caps.

The weather was ideal for walking — sunny with a slight cooling breeze — and we held hands as we absorbed the serenity of our surroundings. Flowers grew along the side of the road as we walked. I picked two and gave them to Faye, placing them in her hair. She smiled and kissed me. The time was so peaceful, I didn't want it to end.

A bridge loomed ahead of us late in the afternoon. It spanned across a wide river flowing from the mountains to the sea. The bank had a steep slope to the water's edge, so I sidestepped to the shore and hand-cupped a sip from it to test it for saltiness. Its coolness poured through my fingers, and a sweet, cool wetness delighted my tongue as I swallowed.

A flat plateau extended nearby, next to the river, grassed and dry, so we set up camp for the night. After setting the tent, I left to collect wood for a fire, leaving Faye to prepare our meal. The surrounding land was sparse of timber, forcing me to hike a distance before recovering enough. As the sun disappeared, the air chilled, so we snuggled by the flames before retiring just before dark.

The next few days followed the same pattern, their serenity the most peaceful of my life. The only blot to the tranquility was our non-progress toward our goal of getting answers.

When our food supplies started dwindling, we headed toward the mountains, hoping to have better luck in locating sustenance. I still carried my homemade spear but hadn't gotten around to finding suitable wood to make a bow or arrows.

We talked of many things as we meandered to our unknown target, my deepening knowledge of Faye increasing her attractiveness. She was becoming a part of me and me of her. We were already pre-empting each other's actions despite the short time we had been together. We laughed when that happened.

We climbed higher and, after several days, entered a forested slope of the mountains. Berries and other edible plants appeared, and I had the fortune of spearing the occasional rabbit. Around midday of one day, we rounded a bend and stumbled on a flat plain by a small brook. A high cliff face rose from the ground and appeared to be chaperoning a stream along its bank.

"Look." I pointed to a hole in the cliff. We wandered over to it.

"It's a cave," Faye said as she moved closer to the opening.

I followed her and stepped inside but stayed near the entrance. After retrieving my flashlight from my bag, I shone the light into the darkness and estimated it to be twenty feet deep; it was dry and unoccupied by animals. The floor comprised rock and a thin film of dirt. Three sturdy rocks rose from the ground at the right height for sitting. One was flat on top and suitable for use as a table. Amused by the coincidental convenience, I looked at Faye and commented as I sat on a stool, "They made this for us."

Faye rested on another. She glanced at me. "Let's stay for a while."

I smiled because I was having the same thought. "Let's."

After dropping our bags, we went and explored our surroundings. I ventured toward the stream and had a drink. The fluid tasted sweet and chilled. We followed the cliff face upstream to explore. The noise of cascades came from up ahead where the ravine disappeared and the brook bent, following it. We rounded the corner to a scene of paradise. Water cascaded from the top of the precipice into a wide pool, exiting via the stream. Ferns and palms populated the slopes by the waterfall and orchid fronds splayed from the odd plant. I put my arm around Faye's waist as we took in the sight. She placed her head on my shoulder and let out a contented sigh as she hugged my waist. We walked to the small lake. It was clear, with a gentle slope as the bottom vanished into darkness a short distance from the edge.

I glanced at Faye, mischief in my mind. "Want a dip?"

She gazed at me, smiling as she saw my intent. "Last one in gets to cook dinner," she yelled as she let go of me and began undressing.

I copied her but lost the race. The lake was frigid as I waded in deep enough to swim with ease. Faye swam over to the falls and rolled over several times as she frolicked just beyond the mist, laughing in delight. I followed her lead. Growing tired, Faye moved to a spot where she could stand, and she rose, flicking her mane back, the clinging liquid spraying behind her. She shimmered in the light as the smooth wetness of her body's upper half emerged from the pool, water dripping from her breasts. A challenging gaze caught me as she stood there, displaying her femininity. That look reeled me in like a fish hooked on an angler's line as I paddled to her and stopped, wiping the liquid from my hair. We closed the gap and kissed. She wrapped both legs around me as she mounted me, and I walked backward into deeper water for balance.

Afterward, we found a grassed spot, settled, and dried off in the sun before dressing again. I can't remember how long we lay there, but I didn't want it to end with her softness and warmth next to me. As we realized we couldn't ignore the reality of tending to our survival, we stood and returned to the cave.

"Welcome to our home," I said.

13

NEW HOME

IT TOOK several days to settle into the cave and explore the surroundings for sources of food. Not only did the pool offer a suitable bathing spot, but it held a large yield of fish. I pondered how they got there. They were a foot to fifteen inches long and were a succulent protein supply. We developed a daily routine: me collecting wood for a fire and meat for a meal; Faye searching for fruit, berries, and root vegetables. She even found a variety of potatoes nearby.

The sun dawned, and we woke to a carefree day. I prepared breakfast, while Faye lingered in bed. She emerged as I placed a serve on the rock table. I devoured my share, but she just stared at hers.

Stopping, I looked at her. "What's wrong? Aren't you hungry?"

"I'm nauseous," she said, staring at her food. She bolted up and rushed from the cave. I heard retching nearby. She returned five minutes later.

I frowned with concern. "Are you alright?"

"I think so. I'm better now, but the odor of the food made me sick."

"That's odd."

"I've never felt that way before."

"Nor have I, unless I've drunk too much, but that doesn't count."

"No, it doesn't," she said, looking at me in disapproval.

I held my hands up in self-defense and replied, "Hey, it won't happen here, will it?"

She sat again and started picking at her food. She frowned. "Am I ill?"

I shrugged. "I don't know. Maybe what we ate last night didn't agree with you."

"You're not affected."

"Might affect people in different ways."

Faye came good later in the morning, and she continued her usual activities.

But the pattern of behavior recurred daily. We both agreed something was amiss. It wasn't getting worse, so we ended up living with it. We could do nothing to cure it.

A couple of weeks afterward, I left for my usual scouting expedition and ventured further up into the mountains. Oaks and alders grew in abundance, and I saw the stream that passed our cave. Willows grew on its banks. I examined the branches for a time and spotted one fit for a bow, so I hacked it off and pared away the leaves and twigs. Once I flexed the branch, I determined it was adaptable for my needs. I studied the tree again and discovered several straight thin offshoots suitable for arrows. I cut them off, too, and continued my trek. Before retracing my steps, I stopped and found a clearing where enormous boulders broke the pattern of trees. They were easy to climb, so I scrambled over them until I reached the highest one and stood on top of it, gazing at the magnificent view. The horizon spread before me in both directions, the sea glistening in the sunlight. As I shaded my eyes, I gazed at the landscape, trying to discern any trace of unnatural objects, buildings, or other structures that would give me a clue of this deity's location. Two sparkling shapes shone in the distance to my left, but they were many days' walk from us. After seeing nothing else of interest, I jumped from the boulders and made my way back to our cave, telling Faye what I had seen. We decided we were too distant to explore the objects for now.

The rumble of a thunderstorm woke me early the next morning. Everything was still pitch black. At least I thought it was night, the murky gloom only disturbed by the occasional sudden and brilliant flash of lightning that lit the cave in blinding light. Rain roared outside like rapids on a river as it hit the tree foliage and the ground. Then dawn came, and the darkness became a wet, ashen gray. The commotion woke Faye, and we cuddled as we listened to the rain's white noise, jumping in fright whenever a thunderclap echoed around us.

I got restless, so I rose and lit a fire at the cave's entrance for both light and heat since a chill hung in the air. With nothing else to do, I started making the bow from the branch I'd brought back and from the cord I'd brought with me, using a length to wrap around the timber for a handgrip. I tested the string's tension with care, and it bowed well without breaking. It withstood the effort I could put into drawing the string backward. Pared arrow points with notches in the other end completed my homemade bow and arrow set, although I knew I needed fletching for the arrows and hoped to find feathers for that purpose.

The thunder and lightning ceased after two hours, but the drenching continued. We stayed in the cave, retiring early when darkness returned.

Sunshine greeted us at dawn. Its sight cheered both our spirits, removing yesterday's depressing atmosphere. I dressed and went to the entrance. Outside, the ground remained wet and the moisture on the leaves glistened in the sunlight. The air smelled fresh as I drew in a lungful in one large breath. Strolling over to the stream, I washed and drank my fill before returning to the cave.

Faye stood in front of me studying her stomach, a frown on her face, as she attempted to zip up her jeans. She looked at me. "Am I getting fat?"

My eyes widened in surprise at the question. "Not that I can tell. Why?"

"My pants are harder to do up as if my waist has expanded."

I shrugged. "Can't see how you'd get big on what we eat."

Faye still frowned but let the topic drop as she breathed in and got her jeans zipped. We both completed our chores and ate breakfast before I ventured off to find feathers and food. Faye said she'd do likewise, so I left her to it while I set out. A dead bird with suitable quills for fletching lay in my path as I walked through the trees, so I collected the quills.

Rabbits inhabited the location, but they remained elusive to trapping. The problem distracted me for an extended time as I pondered different options to skewer, trap, or snare them. Each solution had its difficulties. The creatures weren't fearful of humans, coming near me often, but any sudden movement scared them away. Evidence of carnivores to control the rodent population was missing, although they must prowl the wilds. I rested on a rock thinking over this issue when three rabbits hopped out nearby, only ten feet from me as I stayed still, watching them. They nibbled on grass growing in that spot, biting off a stem or two while scanning their surroundings as their mouths worked to chew the blades. I had my spear leaning on my thigh, and I wondered if I could grab it and move into a throwing position without scaring them. With nothing to lose, I moved at a snail's pace and aimed. The rabbits were oblivious to their present danger from this strange creature that had invaded their territory. After a calming breath, I checked my aim and threw the spear. It caught the nearest one in the stomach, lancing through the body. I smiled in satisfaction as I raced to my catch, picked it up, and slit its throat. Blood dripped out of the wound onto the ground. The rabbit stopped jerking as its life left it. I gutted it but kept the skin on until I returned to the cave.

I traveled across the mountain's slopes and discovered several wild apple trees. They had ripe fruit on them, so I picked a few. With enough to carry, I strolled back to our home, intending to use the rest of the day fletching my arrows and testing the bow.

Faye sat on one of the rock seats in our cave when I returned, staring at nothing, looking worried. "What's wrong?" I asked, as my mood deflated.

She stared at me, fear and uncertainty written on her face. "I might be pregnant."

"What?" I blurted, not because I hadn't heard her, but I didn't understand her words, my eyes wide with surprise.

"I looked up information on the tablet I brought with me. My symptoms suggest I'm pregnant. My nausea and my expanding waist."

I sat on the other rock. "What, you're having a baby?"

"Yes."

I couldn't comprehend what she said. Babies came from ... I didn't know where they originated. They just appeared in the delivery nursery. "How?" I asked.

She smiled, amused at my ignorance. "What do you mean, how? Haven't you seen any nature documentaries on animals? You and me. With our ... amorous activities."

I reddened in embarrassment. Then something dawned on me, and a sense of wonder overpowered me. "A part of us is growing in you?"

Faye nodded. Her worry dissipated, and she smiled. "Yes."

I smiled too as I moved over and kissed her, mulling over the prospect of being a father. Releasing her, I stood straight. Her concern had infected me. How could we care for an infant? When would it come? How? Frowning, I asked, "How do you have a baby?"

"I don't know," Faye said as she shrugged, grimacing. "When the time's right, it comes out through my—"

"A baby can't fit through there surely," I interrupted. "It's too small." I scratched my head. "Isn't it?"

"That's how animals have babies. I presume we do too."

I descended into deep contemplation. "So, with us isolated, we couldn't have offspring this way. It required contact, contrary to the rest of our existence. We needed another reproductive method without humans engaging in sex." I could see why our controller could consider that tidier, more hygienic, easier to manage, and the realization angered me. "That's just plain wrong."

"That may be," Faye said, staring at me. "How will we raise a baby?"

I didn't have an answer for her, so I said, "I caught a rabbit today."

14

BIRTH

THE EXTRA RESPONSIBILITY of bringing a baby into the world weighed heavily on me. Faye saw my worry. She came to me and soothed me at those times, comforting me. I started treating her as if she might break. This half-amused, half-annoyed her, and she would periodically remind me that she was not an invalid. Her bump became noticeable as time passed, and she had problems fitting into her clothes. That depressed her, making it my turn to cheer her up. But her breasts got bigger and neither of us minded that.

In the evenings, we talked about preparing for the baby. It was our obsessive project. From the information on her tablet, Faye gleaned that the human gestation period was nine months, which gave us a temporal target to aim for. Sometimes she became overwhelmed over how long she would have to carry the child and look *fat*, as she called herself.

Keeping track of time became a necessity. From the outset, we had both been keeping a rough diary of our daily activities on the tablet. But now we made sure we recorded something every day, which made it easier to tally up the passing weeks and months.

Another issue came to light, too. With the pregnancy, Faye started tiring more often and with less effort. She couldn't forage for food as she used to, requiring me to labor twice as hard to cater for us both. I seldom returned with enough and would let her eat what she needed first, leaving me hungry most days. She saw my hunger and protested, but I told her it was for the baby and endured it.

My bow and arrows required several modifications before they were an efficient killing machine, but I eventually became proficient in hunting for rabbits and birds with them. I kept the rabbit skins and dried them, thinking of using them for baby clothes. We discussed making cotton or wool material, but we didn't know how to. No cotton or other plants for thread grew nearby, and there certainly weren't any sheep.

Sometimes I climbed the mountains and gazed with longing toward the mysterious reflections in the distance, eager to discover what they were, but we couldn't leave the cave. Had we been wrong about leaving our complex? Guilt consumed me over making Faye suffer from my obsession with finding this entity.

One day, I returned to our home with two rabbits, a tuber, and berries. They would make a sumptuous meal for a change. I skinned the animals and let them sit on a rock while I got the fire going, skewering them on spits I'd constructed to cook them over the embers. I looked at Faye as I squatted, tending to the rabbits. Her advanced pregnancy, her belly bulbous, amazed me.

"Quick, come here," she said.

Panicking, I rushed over to her. "What's wrong?"

"Here, place your hand on my stomach," she said as she grabbed it and guided it there.

I frowned in confusion, but as I flattened my palm over the spot she steered it to, I felt a tapping against it. My eyes widened. "What's that?"

Faye smiled. "I think it's kicking."

Staring at my hand again, I experienced the occasional thumping taps against it with wonder. It was strong and seemingly intentional, and tears trickled down my cheeks. I suddenly remembered the rabbits and returned to rotate them, looking back at Faye with the memory of the kicks sending a sense of awe into my soul.

We had a satisfying meal that night, and Faye and I sat in the firelight late, content in each other's arms. I rubbed her stomach, wondered how much larger her abdomen could grow, and considered how long she had been pregnant. We estimated she must be over half-way. The prospect of another three to four months depressed Faye, but she snapped out of it as I soothed her belly with my rubbing.

I had an extensive beard by now. I'd always been clean-shaven in the complex, but now, without the proper shaving equipment, it has been too difficult. Faye said the beard made me look distinguished, but I just looked at her, doubting her sincerity.

Days passed, each melding into another with little discernible change, apart from Faye's stomach imperceptibly growing larger. I continued with my hunting and gathering and found enough to prevent starvation — some days, bringing back feasts and other days leaving what I collected for Faye to eat. I would lie and say I had eaten things while I was away.

Our estimate of nine months approached, and Faye held her hips as she waddled most days, counterbalancing the weight of the child. It kicked often, and I often felt the kicks as I lay next to Faye.

I woke one morning like every other and prepared to go hunting.

Faye stirred. "Something's different."

"What?"

"I don't know. Something's unusual with the baby. I don't want you to leave me."

"But I have to get food," I protested, although we had a small supply of emergency dried fruits we had accumulated.

Faye looked at me, worried and pleading, and I knew I had to obey her appeal. So, instead of going hunting, I collected wood nearby and completed other neglected tasks. My gaze lingered on her with concern when I returned to the cave. I left for a longer period on the chance of finding food, which I did by stumbling across a berry bush in fruit, and with luck, I stumbled on a rabbit, which I killed. I heard Faye groan as I walked back. Alert to a problem, I ran the rest of the way. "What is it?"

Faye looked at me, her face fearful. "I think it's coming. I'm getting pain spasms." Several minutes later, she groaned again, and a gush of liquid flowed down her legs.

I stared in panic. "What do I do?"

"You need to relax," she said.

Flapping my arms around, as if that would solve everything, I rushed outside and then returned.

"Will you stop that?" Faye asked, a wry smile accompanying her creased brow. "You're making me nervous. Go get that rabbit-fur ground cover you made so I can lie on it."

"Yeah ... sure," I said as I stared at her and blinked. I ran off and brought the rug back, placing it on the floor in a sheltered part of the cave away from our usual activities. I looked at her, worried, but with a measure of excitement, too.

Faye groaned again and bowed over in pain. She straightened as the spasm subsided and leaned against the wall with her hand. She glanced at me. "Can you heat water so I can wash my legs?"

I jumped to do her bidding and started a fire, putting a pot on it. After it boiled, I put a quantity into a bowl with cold water and brought it into her. My ears were alert and pricked up every time I heard her groan again. Her pain seemed to come at ten-minute intervals. She remained standing when I returned, shuffling around in between contractions. I used a rag to wash her legs with gentle strokes as she stood. She smiled at me in appreciation when I finished, just before bending over, suffering from another contraction.

"Shouldn't you lie down?"

"No, it's better walking." She waddled from one end of the cave to the other but always near a rock or wall that she could lean on.

Watching her in her misery made me feel useless. I was so unprepared for this event. And yet it gave me a sense of being alive. This had never happened in the complex. The pain Faye endured looked terrible, but it was pain she would never have encountered. Does that make isolation better? It was, in one sense, but I couldn't help but conclude that this experience was part of being human.

The day wore on, with little more happening than Faye's spasms of agony. Her contractions increased in frequency and intensity by late afternoon. She started screaming as her pain intensified, leaving me staring in futility about what I should do, could do, to help her. I fetched her food to eat and gave her water to quench her thirst. Beads of perspiration appeared on her forehead as she cussed and cursed her suffering. She gave way to her need for rest and lay on the rug, and I sat next to her with a damp cloth to wipe her brow. I held her hand at one stage but soon realized my mistake when she had another contraction and crushed it in hers.

Modesty had no home here. She stretched, legs spread, with her knees up, her dress folded back above her waist, and wearing no underwear. The contractions became less than five minutes apart as the sun started setting. Faye's pain, as she screamed on and on, seemed unbearable until the spasm relented, only to regroup for another campaign. She breathed in rapid puffs as she gathered her strength for the next bout.

I made a fire closer to the cave mouth to give light, as I suspected the birthing would continue after dark. Coming back to her with more warm water, I noticed her vagina dilated larger than I had ever seen it and stood staring at it.

"Haven't you seen that before?" Faye asked when she caught me looking.

"Not like this. Maybe the baby is coming."

Faye glanced down but saw nothing with the baby's mound blocking her view. She probed the spot with her hand before another contraction overpowered her. It was difficult seeing in the encroaching darkness, but the dilation increased with each contraction. I nervously approached and peered closer. "I can see something." Excitement overtook my concern. "It's almost out." I smiled at her.

"It damn well better be," Faye said as another contraction began.

The circle grew larger. "One more push."

Wiping Faye's brow again and encouraging her with a squeeze of her hand, I looked at her. She gazed back, frightened, but seemed to hold a sense of hope that the birth would soon end. Another contraction began, and I dashed to see. The crown of the baby's head appeared as Faye yelled in agony. "Push more," I said, trying to encourage her. She gave one more scream as the blood vessels in her neck protruded. More head showed, and then its eyes, nose, and mouth. Then the entire head emerged while Faye screamed at the top of her voice, her lungs seeming to burst. I moved between Faye's legs and supported the baby's head as its shoulders appeared, and then the rest just seemed to flow out. Suddenly, I was holding a newborn in my hands with the umbilical cord snaking back into Faye. The baby coughed and started crying, bringing tears of joy. Faye lay exhausted on the mat. She peered at me with a fulfilled smile. "It's a boy," I said.

"You need to cut the cord and tie it off," she said.

"Oh." I laid the infant on the mat and got my knife, cutting the umbilical cord and tying as Faye said. I then lifted the child and took him to her, so she could hold him. She reached out and wrapped her arms around him as she let him rest on her chest, laughing and crying at the same time.

The boy started moving as though trying to find something. "Quick, get my dress up further. I think he wants to drink." I helped raise her garment above her breasts. The baby latched onto Faye's nipple with his mouth, sucking, even though there didn't seem to be anything to suck. It would be another day, we would learn, before the milk in Faye's engorged breasts came down, enabling the baby to feed.

I cleaned up the child as it suckled. "You did it," I said as I wiped the blood and other fluid away.

Faye looked back at me, exhausted, but beaming with happiness. "Yes, we did."

The placenta came out an hour later, and I buried it straightaway, according to the instructions on the tablet.

"What do you want to call him?" Faye asked when the baby had fallen asleep on her stomach.

That was a good question. We hadn't considered it, not knowing if it would be a boy or a girl. After dwelling on it for a minute, I suggested, "How about Adam?"

15

RETURN?

ADAM'S BIRTH PREOCCUPIED ME. New tasks ate into my working day of hunting and gathering. This included constructing a small cradle from branches I lined with rabbit skins. I was proud of my resourcefulness, and Adam seemed comfortable when we lay him in it. Faye and I smiled with pride as we watched him, holding hands, while he slept. We had to work out his toiletry habits to keep him (and us) clean. It took inventiveness, but we found a rabbit pelt solution. I scraped off their fur and softened them so they wouldn't chafe Adam as he moved. We had the odd *accidents,* and we cussed and laughed when that happened. The responsibility was tough, but we learned to cope. Both Faye and I had tantrums of frustration, but fortunately, not at the same time.

I came back from my hunting one afternoon with a successful supply of food: a rabbit and several tubers and apples. My success encouraged me to try for a fish in the pool by the waterfall, and I speared one. After cleaning the fish and skinning the rabbit, I cooked them, and we sat by the fire eating the food to our fill for a change. Adam sat in Faye's lap as we ate, eyes gaping at us as our movements caught his attention. I poked my finger toward him, playing a grab-it game. Adam was uncoordinated and struggled to participate, but he smiled as we played. We both laughed at him when he thrashed his arms out to snatch my digit. He started crying after a while, so Faye fed him while I cleaned up and packed away leftovers.

She sat next to me, contemplating, after Adam fell asleep. I sat by the fire, gazing out at the forest and stream. "This is nowhere to raise a kid," she said.

I looked at her, surprised by the topic, and frowned. We had limited options from my perspective, but I wanted to know her thoughts. She was right, of course. Our current lifestyle was inappropriate to bring up a child. Not only were we living as primitives, but Adam would miss social interaction with other children if we stayed and did nothing. He wouldn't get to enjoy the world's technology and luxuries, either, or have a proper education. "What are your views?" she asked me.

"I don't know. Should we go back?"

"That's not possible. Would you want to return to our old living arrangements? They'd separate us from each other and from Adam. And I don't want Adam taken away from me. That's cruel to him. He'll notice something's changed, and he will suffer."

"We wouldn't even get our old apartments back," Faye continued. "Somebody else has them by now, I bet. But it's inappropriate raising Adam this way, too, scrounging for food every day. He doesn't have any clothes, apart from what we can pull together from rabbit skins. I don't want him to live like this. Who's he going to socialize with as he grows? And what if he gets sick?"

Faye's concern was palpable, and I shared it. I just didn't have adequate answers for her. I sat in thought while Faye put her hand in mine and leaned on my shoulder.

"If we can't go back," I said finally, "and we can't stay like this, then we have to move forward and continue our search."

It would be disappointing to leave the cave's shelter and security, but we lived in limbo with no purpose at present. If we could locate this entity and ask it why we lived like we did and convince it to give us refuge and an apartment where we could be together, I'd then be happier with that idea than returning to nothing or living outside our society. I suppose people might say it serves us right for leaving what we had, but they haven't had our experiences. Deciding, I said to Faye, "We should investigate those other structures I saw on the horizon."

"But they're so far away," she said, wide-eyed and frightened.

"We might find answers. And a better life for Adam."

Faye stared at me with an unconvinced look but had no alternative to suggest. "I'll consider it," she said.

We retired to bed after that.

Faye started foraging for food soon afterward. We made up a sling to carry Adam in while we walked. She became happier being active again, especially as it improved her fitness. Still, Adam kept her occupied for a large part of the day.

I left, as usual, one morning after our talk and wandered into the mountains, threading my way through the forest in search of rabbits. Two showed later in the day, and I speared one with an arrow. I was an expert archer now, after much experience. I returned to the rocky outcrop, where I sat and studied the glimmer in the distance, feeling the mystery drawing me to it. Our predicament hadn't resurfaced in our discussions again, but we had to decide soon. It was getting late, so I started strolling back to the cave.

I fronted a tree to urinate and began relieving myself when I sensed an object in the branches overhead. Thinking it was a bird, I looked up, but my mouth gaped open. A small drone hovered amongst the leaves. An unobtrusive blinking light on its front drew my attention. It moved to hide, but insufficient foliage prevented its concealment. What was it doing here? It carried no weapons like the factory drones. It just lingered, as if spying on me, scaring me. The entity must have discovered our relocation. But why? Why take an interest in us now? After finishing my business, I couldn't figure out what to do. It drifted, frozen where it was as I looked at it. A panicky dread overpowered me. *What if it has located Faye and Adam? What if it has taken them away?* As I recovered from my stasis, I raced back to our home, crashing through the brush as I ran. I stopped several times to see if it followed me, but after gasping for a few breaths, I started running again, desperate to return.

Breaking through the last bushes, I sped to our cave, and a bemused Faye stared at me as she walked with Adam in her arms, trying to get him to sleep. I bent to catch my breath before speaking, perspiration dripping from me. "I saw a drone," I said.

Faye's smile vanished. "What?"

"I was taking a ... relieving myself and got distracted. A drone—." I looked up and around, searching for it. Looking back at Faye, I continued, "It just hovered with a blinking light. It was trying to hide amongst the leaves. It's spying on us."

Faye's eyes darted between the baby and me, fear in them. "Do you think it's been doing that for long? Has it discovered this cave?"

"I don't know."

"What are we going to do?"

"I don't know. What does it mean? It knows we're alive now." I paused, lost in thought. "They should have a limited range. We must investigate its origin and communicate with whoever sent it. We have to leave."

16

THE CITY

FAYE AGREED we needed to discover the drone's home. If the object had spied my movements, it likely still hovered in the region. With any luck, it might follow us, or even lead us, if the entity controlling it wanted us at a specific place. We packed our belongings, adapted one of our duffle bags into a harness so we could take turns carrying Adam, and were on our way. We both felt sad to leave what had become our home for almost a year, but we had to move on, for Adam's sake, if nothing else.

Once we crossed the river, we traveled north and east, winding our way out of the woodland and onto grassland, bare of edible vegetation. The forest had served us well, but it receded behind us and left us in a quandary as to whether we should journey through the plain, hoping for more promising terrain, or consider another route north. We carried a supply of food, but it would soon dwindle without replenishment. Once we decided on continuing through the grass, we set up camp as the sun set in the western sky. Our other problem was the lack of wood for a fire, so we had to settle for a quick meal and retire before darkness fell upon us, although a plump crescent moon and cloudless skies provided good visibility.

Adam seemed to consider the trek an adventure, giving little trouble apart from the usual grumbles for food and toiletry concerns, smiling and gaping at the sights and sounds. The walking sway sent him to sleep. His growth amazed me. He sprouted in front of our eyes, and his perception and interaction had improved since he was born. Faye and I enjoyed playing with him as he goo-ed and gaa-ed and smiled.

The sun rose the next day, and I left our tent early to find food and water. I stumbled on two rabbits in my wandering, but with no means of cooking them, I let them be. After searching for half an hour, I surrendered to its futility and returned to Faye as she finished feeding Adam. I had a quick bite to eat and packed up, getting us on our way soon afterward.

The countryside changed after midday, as did the weather. Shrubs populated our path, increasing our hopes of finding more food. But clouds rolled across the sky. We stumbled on a stream mid-afternoon and debated whether we should stay or continue. The weather's deterioration made our minds up for us, and we pitched the tent by the watercourse before I started my search for food. Wood littered the ground, so I collected a pile to make a fire later. Rabbits hopped into view upstream as dusk approached, and I caught one, which pleased me. Not seeing any berries or any other edible vegetation, I returned and prepared the fire, cooking the rabbit. Faye had located berries as she walked with Adam while I was away. She shared them with me.

The sky looked dreary and threatening, so I stoked the fire with more wood and tended the cooking rabbit, hoping it would be ready to eat before it rained. Drops started falling just as I removed the rabbit from the heat and let it cool, placing more timber on the embers to support its combustion in the rain. It popped and sizzled as drops fell into the burning coals. A steady downpour began and extinguished the flames, so we consumed the rabbit and retired.

Our journey continued in a similar vein for another five days. Finding enough food to sustain us was our chief occupation. I made sure Faye ate. We started our trekking on the sixth day like the others. The sun was out and warm, and the landscape became undulating. Midmorning, we crested a rise and stopped.

"What is this?" Faye asked.

"Good question."

The terrain fell into a long valley, and buildings stood throughout, worn-out skeletons ready to collapse into a well-earned pile of rest. They were unlike the constructions we were used to, as they were small and lined up along crisscrossing laneways of ground, weeds growing here and there. A river flowed through the center of the conglomeration.

"They're ancient buildings," I said. "Let's go have a look."

We descended into the valley and entered the metropolis, peeking into the structures as we passed. Most looked purposed for residences, the remains of rusted beds and collapsed tables occupying many of them. Other buildings were shops and other places of commerce. We gaped at the place.

"I wonder where the people went?" Faye frowned at the unusual sight.

"To the complexes, maybe."

We rounded the corner of a building and saw one with a cross on it, half hanging sideways, ready to fall. A plot of land lay next to it, retreating a long way, with rows and rows of stones standing upright. Looking at Faye, I shrugged, and we walked over to see what they were. Carved writing appeared as we neared a slab: an epitaph and a person's name and dates. It sent shivers down my spine. The others were similar as we wandered, many with similar dates of death. I scratched my head. "They buried dead people here."

"Why do that?"

"I don't know. Tradition years ago?"

"And a lot of them died around the same time."

"This is giving me the creeps. Let's get away from here."

"It's getting late in the day. Let's find shelter to sleep. A building near the stream."

Faye agreed, so we ventured toward the river and searched in a few buildings before we found one that was sturdy and weatherproof. The door screeched as I opened it and fell off its hinges. Cobwebs hung everywhere. Faye looked on in trepidation, but I stepped in and swept them away, waving my spear, clearing a space we could occupy. Glassless windows let in the fading light from the outside, giving us visibility of the interior. I explored the other rooms. One was a bathroom with taps, a ceramic bath, basin, and toilet bowl. I tried the taps, but they remained unmoved, seized. Nothing there was of value to us. Faye sat on the floor in the first room with Adam when I returned, playing with him, and she glanced up and smiled at me as he grasped her fingers with his tiny hands.

"I might search for firewood and food before it gets dark," I said. Faye nodded, and I walked out into the town again. Timber from the buildings lay scattered throughout the place, most of it rotted into uselessness. Enough remained for me to light a fire, leaving me with finding items to eat.

I headed in the graveyard's direction at the edge of the township. The river flowed through the town's center, and vegetation encroached from the surrounds. I carried my bow and arrows and my spear in case I saw a rabbit or another animal to catch. Luck was on my side. Three rabbits congregated by the river's waterline where shrubs camouflaged them. Several trees stood near the bank, which provided a good hiding spot for me to watch them while I considered which one gave me the best opportunity. With no need to move closer than the shrubs, I aimed and shot the closest rabbit with an arrow through the chest, giving it a quick death. The others ran off when they realized the lurking danger. I picked up the rabbit and cut its neck, looking around as I let the blood drip out. My eyes caught sight of a blinking light by the building with the cross, three hundred feet away. A drone hovered in the air. So, it was following us, or this was a different one. Something was keeping track of what we were doing. *Who is spying on us? Is the drone providing a live feed to the base? Or is it storing the information for later analysis?* I wished I knew, and I wished I knew the base's location. The drone looked too fast to follow.

It was getting dark, so I strode back to the house and prepared the rabbit for cooking, informing Faye of the drone. She looked scared, but I reassured her it didn't intend to harm us or it would have already harmed us. The fire roasted the rabbit, and we ate before darkness fell for the night. Faye fed the baby before we both settled for slumber. Scuttling noises disturbed us before we could sleep.

"What's that?" Faye whispered, holding me tight. A squeaking sounded nearby.

I listened to figure out what it could be. "It's nothing. Go to sleep."

"I can't sleep with that sneaking around the room."

"It doesn't sound very large."

Faye lay still but kept hold of my arm as I settled. We heard it a few more times before the house returned to silence and we fell asleep.

A loud noise woke me at one stage. It was pitch black, but I saw a light. Creeping from our sleeping bag, I slinked over to the window to peer out. A set of lights was coming toward me in the distance. The roar grew louder, waking Faye. "What is it?" she asked, rubbing her eyes as she bent to a sitting position. "I hope it doesn't wake up Adam."

"I don't know." The lights brightened, and the din increased until they passed the house and out of view. "It's a truck," I said. "This must be one of their routes."

"What's it doing running around at night?" Faye complained.

Adam started crying.

Faye groaned in the darkness.

17

NOMADS

As LUCK HAD IT, the truck traveling through the city just before dawn brightened the eastern horizon. Faye fed Adam, and he settled straight away, giving her relief and time to catch whatever sleep possible before having to rise. I stayed up and dressed, strolling to the river to wash my face.

Birds sang in the trees to greet the new day, their familiar chortling reminiscent of our stay at the cave. I listened and distinguished three or four different calls as they crooned to each other. The chatter warmed my heart. I had never experienced such a thing while imprisoned in my apartment, although I could have gone for a PR walk in an open space at dawn if I'd chosen. Walking along the river, I found a bush with berries on it. I picked a supply to take back. A woodland lay ahead, so I continued in that direction, and luck provided an apple tree in fruit with bright red apples. I took them, stuffing them in my pockets, careful not to bruise them. I ate one on my way back to Faye.

"Catch," I said, throwing an apple at her.

She yelped but caught it, giving me a frown with a smirk afterward.

"These should last a few days," I said, unloading my supplies.

"Maybe we can pick more before we leave," Faye responded. "I'm going to the river. You look after Adam." She walked off, humming to herself.

Adam still slept, so I had a peaceful time by myself. He was a well-behaved baby, rarely complaining and mostly sleeping through the night. Another truck rolled through soon after Faye left, and I ate a handful of berries and another apple. I leaned in the doorway, thinking of what we should do as I continued taking bites from the fruit. A hissing behind me disturbed my concentration, and I turned to investigate the sound. My eyes widened when I saw a monstrous feral cat standing near Adam's cradle, looking at him and then at me with evil intent. My heart raced in alarm as I ran over to Adam and chased the beast away. It held its ground at first but retreated when I got too close. That was the first wild cat I had seen.

Faye returned, and I told her about the cat, making her panic for Adam's safety. There was nothing for us in the town, so we ate, fed Adam, and continued our journey to a place unknown, deciding to follow the lorry transport route as the most likely way of reaching our goal. It made it easy to cross rivers and other land-based obstructions, the road providing access for the lorries to traverse the landscape. We collected more apples before we left and stashed them wherever they would fit without bruising. By the time we finished eating them, we were sick of the sight of apples.

The highway meandered through the countryside but veered to the coast in the end, hugging it. We traveled through various terrains, sometimes open grassland, other times wooded areas and impressive forests, with mighty trees towering overhead. Although it tried to stay unobserved, I detected the drone studying us but ignored it, given that it was otherwise ignoring us.

We took Adam into the sea when the road went nearby. At first, the seawater ebbing and flowing over the shallow sand confused him, but it soon entertained him, and he laughed in delight when the water poured over his chubby legs. Faye looked at me as she held him, and I smiled with joy at their fun.

I continued catching rabbits, and we fed ourselves with enough supplies to prevent starvation, although our stomachs grumbled when food was scarce.

Adam's arrival had tamed our amorosity. We still enjoyed sex often, but we kept tabs on Faye's menstrual cycle, now that we knew more about it and what it signified, timing our intimacy to suit. We didn't want a second child to look after under our current circumstances. Despite that, our relationship grew closer and deeper, and I couldn't imagine life without Faye anymore. I marveled at the strange coincidence that had brought her into my world and how perfect she was for me as if a cosmic force had drawn us together.

I remember one night when the sky was cloudless and the stars bright, we camped in the grass just off the beach and I lay down in front of a blazing fire after our meal. I felt a deep content as I gazed at the twinkling lights, marveling at their distance. Orion sparkled overhead.

Faye came and settled next to me. "What are you thinking?" she asked, a contented smile on her face as she snuggled up to me.

I glanced at her and smiled back, returning my gaze to the sky. "I was just wondering if we will ever fly to the stars someday, or whether they'll be forever beyond our reach."

"Could we travel there in our PR world?"

Her inquiry puzzled me. It was an interesting and probing one, considering the unknown limits of PR technology. I frowned. "Good question. I don't think so. I've never heard that it's a possibility. They've never asked me to program such a scenario. They taught us you can't travel faster than the speed of light. So, it'd take centuries to fly to even the closest stars. Who'd live in PR for years?"

"Go into suspended animation?"

"What would happen to your body, then? The whole conception relies on your actual body functioning. It'd be fraught with danger."

"Pity."

I glanced at Faye to see if she was making fun of me, but she looked sincere and accepted my analysis. She shone like a goddess in the starlight, so I rolled over and kissed her, stroking her hair as we stared into each other's eyes afterward. I wanted to stay in that position forever, but Adam woke and started crying. We both laughed and sighed, and Faye rose to tend to his needs while I gazed at the stars for a few moments more before I, too, returned to our tent.

Adam grew so fast that I soon had to adjust his crib length and clothing so he continued to fit in both. I wished we had decent clothes for him, but we had to improvise with what we had. He became more aware of the world around him, and he gave both of us much joy as he developed.

The day after our study of the stars began with typical monotony. I packed while Faye tended to Adam, and we started along the road again. The wind picked up during the morning with a chill forewarning of a change in the weather. Clouds gathered and filled the sky soon after, threatening rain, but it held off for the time being. The terrain became undulating, and the route wound through a gully between two elevations. They weren't cliffs, but they were steep, treeless, and covered with grass, and we continued following the road's meandering path.

A junction lay ahead as we rounded a bend, forcing us to consider which way we might take, but we waited until we reached the intersection before deciding. In the end, it wasn't much of a decision. One direction led to more countryside. The other led to a complex of structures in a large valley. I looked at Faye and she me. We both nodded and headed for the buildings.

18

THE COMPOUND

THE BUILDINGS TOWERED over us as we approached them. They were concrete structures with no windows that we could see, although they appeared to have ventilation slots at regular intervals. The main building was enormous. Four other smaller structures surrounded it. A ten-foot-high wall encircled them with a gated entrance where the road entered the compound. I found it odd that the gate was open.

"What are these?" Faye asked.

I shrugged. "Don't know. Are we expected? Let's find a door."

Faye looked frightened as she stood with Adam strapped to her chest, looking at me.

"We won't go in, not yet."

Considering it safe, she walked closer to the largest building and strolled along the walls with me. "It's not a residential compound," she observed.

As we approached the far end, four huge pipes, six feet in diameter, supported on concrete pedestals and piercing the enclosing fence, came into view. They entered the wall of the main building. They were high enough for us to walk under as we continued our exploration. Three metal doors penetrated the long wall. Two provided personal access, but the other was twenty feet high and wide. They resembled sliding panels but remained closed when we neared them. I didn't want to try them at present. We completed our circuit and circumnavigated the other buildings. They were of similar construction except they didn't have conduits entering them; they had one large and one smaller door each. There was no shelter we could use for accommodation within the compound.

"We should hang around here. See if there's any action in here," I suggested as I continued inspecting the buildings, confused over their purpose. They looked important, but their exterior gave no clues as to why.

"I don't want to stay inside the fence," Faye said. "The gate might shut and we'd be trapped."

"We'd climb over it, but I get your point." I glanced up, checking for drones but couldn't see any. "Let's find a place nearby to set up camp."

After leaving the compound, we walked the wall perimeter, scouting for a suitable location. Our greatest need was proximity to a source of freshwater. As we rounded the rear of the fencing, we saw a large river pierce the hills, hemming in the valley. It flowed through part of it and retreated through another gap in the surrounding hills. The four conduits disappeared below the surface. We strolled to the bank for a closer inspection. They plunged into the water; their ends were obscured by their depth. I touched each pipe and the two downstream walls felt warmer than the ones upstream, but I didn't understand the phenomenon's significance.

Several trees lined the riverbanks on both sides, and a copse surrounded a small indent in the hills. "Let's look over there," I said, pointing to the indent. Faye nodded and followed me as I led the way. We saw the grove had bushes scattered throughout the woods, and they were laden with fruit we were familiar with and was edible, if somewhat tasteless. As we threaded our way through, we discovered a rocky outcrop with a massive protruding ledge. Underneath was hollow and six feet from the ground, providing a large, sheltered placement ideal for us to set up our camp for a while.

Faye agreed. She dropped the bag she carried and took Adam from his harness. I did likewise, and she gave Adam to me while she removed the harness and rubbed the areas where the straps chafed her skin. I erected the tent and unpacked our items before telling Faye I wanted to collect wood and left. The copse had wind-damaged tree branches lying on the ground I could break up and use. I had a heaped pile before long and stopped collecting when I considered I had several days' worth. Faye fed Adam as I went back and forth. She strolled with him over her shoulder when I finished, coaxing any residual reflux from him. He gave a large burp when I looked at him, which made me laugh. Fortunately for Faye, nothing else exited his mouth.

"Can you tend to him?" Faye asked as she gave him to me and started walking away. "I want to have a wash in the river."

"Sure you don't want me to help?" I responded with a leering grin.

She glanced back at me and smiled. "I'm sure."

I redirected my attention to Adam. "Well, what are your thoughts on this?" I asked him as I sat and placed him on my legs in a sitting position.

He stared at me with inquisitive and wide eyes, as if considering his reply. He flared his arms. "Gooo ..." came from his mouth as he gave a gummy smile.

"I agree."

"Ga, ga, ga, gaaa ..."

"You don't say?" I laughed. He looked so happy and carefree, oblivious to the hardships we endured. We were fortunate that Faye had ample milk for his needs and that we were finding enough food for her to continue providing it. I reached out and grabbed hold of his hand, stroking it with my thumb. He stared at it and tried pulling back, but I held it a moment longer before releasing it, and he flapped his arm, slapping mine as if to chastise me. Grabbing both his hands, I jiggled my knees, lifting Adam and letting him stay suspended in midair before his weight dropped him onto my legs again. He screamed with delight.

A loud noise broke from his rear end moments before the familiar sweet smell hit my nostrils. I cringed. "That's why Mommy left us then," I said to Adam as I resigned myself to cleaning him. I placed him on the ground, searched through our belongings, and retrieved a rug we used for the purpose, rags for wiping him, and a replacement makeshift diaper — a rabbit skin with the fur on the exterior surface. I needed to wash the old one in the river when Faye returned. We had argued initially over the responsibility for the chore but settled on the premise that the person who changed the nappy cleaned it. The mess wasn't disastrous, so I wiped his bottom and put the fresh lining on him, thankful I didn't have to take him to the stream to give him a decent rinse. The used one remained by a tree until Faye came back. After playing with him a while longer, he started getting tired and grizzly, so I picked him up and rocked him to sleep just as Faye appeared.

"I missed the fun," Faye said as she looked at the soiled skin.

I gave her a feigned glare. "You knew that was coming."

She laughed. "Oh, you poor darling. Give him to me so you can do the rest of your task."

"I just got him to doze. We'll wake him if you take him."

Faye folded her arms. "Nice try."

I pouted my lips, frowned, and sighed as I handed Adam over to her. Once I picked up the soiled nappy, I strode to the river and washed it, washing my face afterward to freshen myself, and I had a draft of water while I was at it. Faye had him in his cot when I returned.

It was midafternoon, and I wanted to scout around for food before nightfall, so I left her with Adam and explored our surroundings, especially the hillside and by the river, hoping rabbits populated the region. They were in abundance everywhere else. Other rocky outcrops scarred the hills, and I ventured over to them, scaling their rough sculptured lines to the top. An outcrop provided footing to climb to a towering height, giving me a view of the countryside, both toward the mysterious compound and away from it. When I reached the hilltop, I noticed a large woodland extended into the distance. Feeling venturous, I strolled to the trees to explore their surrounds. Many bushes were mixed in with the trees as I wandered through the shadows. A brook flowed through the woods, and I wondered if it connected with the river because it sloped that way. Movement caught my eye as I dawdled toward the stream and a sudden noise caused me to freeze and gaze in the noise's direction. Three rabbits hopped to the creek, oblivious to my presence. My long practiced stealthy movements allowed me to kill one of them with an arrow, now happy we had a meal for the night. I bled the rabbit and gutted it, impaling it on the spear to carry back to the camp. Two familiar shrubs grew near the bank. They were thorny, and I recognized blackberries growing on them, so I picked a pouchful. The sun was low in the sky when I strode to our tent and skinned the rabbit, making a fire afterward and setting up a rig to roast the rabbit over the flames.

Faye and I sat by the campfire as we ate the remains of the rabbit, licking our fingers in a well-practiced ritual. I drew my knees up and wrapped my arms around them, feeling relaxed and at peace with the world for now. Darkness crept over the landscape, and the stars emerged as I stared into the flames, throwing another piece of timber into it when the blaze decreased.

A familiar blue blinking light caught my eye through the foliage as I gazed out into the trees. "Faye?"

"What?"

"Over there. It's back spying on us again."

She looked to where I stared. "Oh. I wonder whether it comes from that compound."

"It must have a home somewhere nearby. Although, given where we've seen it, it has a significant range."

"So long as it keeps its distance. It gives me the creeps."

19

CAPTURE

Clouds overcast the sky the next morning, and a slight breeze blew with a chill in it before the sun started heating the air. I blinked and peered over to Faye, who still slept, her rhythmic breathing just audible. I enjoyed watching her sleep, looking at her natural elegance in its relaxed state. She looked exhausted, though, and I didn't blame her, as she'd had to attend to Adam several times during the night, which was unusual. Careful not to wake her, I rose and left for the stream to wash my face and drink the fresh cool liquid. As I walked along the shoreline, I came to a small backwater where the river eddied, leaving the water calm and transparent. The overhead strata reflected from the surface, but I saw fish lazily swipe their tails from side to side as they swam between the reeds. I uttered a curse for not having my spear with me and glanced back to our camp, wondering if it was worthwhile returning to retrieve it. On deciding it was, I jogged to get it. Faye still slumbered, and Adam wriggled in his crib, smacking his lips together as if he were eating something as he dreamed.

I trotted back to the spot with the fish and watched. They continued to flit through the reeds in their leisurely way. With my spear gripped in my hand, I stared into the water, undecided which fish to throw it at as they moved into view. After cursing myself for my procrastination, one drifted straight toward me, so I took aim and thrust the harpoon into the stream, the familiar resistance as the tip pierced the flesh reporting success. I lifted the shaft with a wriggling and jerking foot-long fish impaled on it. It gulped its demise on the riverbank. I gutted it before returning to our camp again, eager to get a fire going to cook it.

Faye had stirred while I was away, and she stood gazing at Adam as I approached. "Hi," I said.

She looked up and smiled. "Hi." When she noticed the fish, she raised her brow. "Breakfast?"

"Yeah. How you feeling? You had a busy night."

"Alright. I'll survive." She frowned. "It's unusual for him. Hope there's nothing wrong with him."

"He looks healthy to me." I left to start the fire and prepared the food for cooking. Faye departed to wash while I cooked the meat on the embers.

The sun peeked from between a gap in the clouds, mottling the landscape as I gazed toward the river and the unnatural compound of structures in the distance. There was no point in returning to explore the site further, as we knew we couldn't enter any buildings, and there was nothing else of interest. Adam's grizzling caught my attention as I pondered our future, so I went to tend to his needs. His eyes were wide open, and he wriggled his arms and kicked his legs in his crib, staring at me as I peered at him. I lifted him. "How are you this morning, my mighty warrior?" I played with his hand with my finger. He gave a gurgling response as if acknowledging my greeting. He looked so happy, I brought him back to the fire and put him on the grass nearby while I inspected the fish. It wasn't ready, so I kept playing with Adam.

Faye soon returned, and Adam goo-ed with excitement at seeing her. She laughed in delight. "You hungry too? What happened last night?" she said as she squatted and rubbed Adam's stomach with her fingers. He responded with noises of joy as his arms and legs worked overtime, making both of us laugh.

My confined life came to me in a flash of confusion and sadness. "Can you imagine this happening where we were? I don't just mean caring for ourselves, but this sensuality of touch with Adam. I've never experienced the intimacy of it ... the humanness if that's a word. It makes me sad. The others will never experience it."

Faye turned her head and looked back at me, a residual smile lingering. "No. We couldn't have these experiences in that prison. We've sacrificed so much comfort and luxury by leaving, but I'd do it again in an instant, for these moments." She returned her attention to Adam and resumed tickling his stomach, generating the same response.

I checked the fish. It was ready, so I removed it and put it on a rabbit-pelt leather mat to cool. Once its temperature dropped to an edible range, I peeled off the skin and pulled off flakes of flesh as the aroma tantalized my nostrils. The rich river-seasoned taste burst in my mouth as I ate it. I picked more flesh off and took it to Faye in my fingers. She grabbed my hand and drew the flesh from my fingers as she placed them sensuously into her mouth, her eyes teasing me as she licked the residual fat from them afterward, challenging me to other thoughts. I groaned with pleasure, but Adam brought us both back to reality when he started grizzling as if protesting this distraction from our focus on him.

Frowning, Faye returned her attention to him and sighed, as she knew the sound meant he was hungry, too. She picked him up and retreated to her resting spot to feed him. I continued eating my share of fish, leaving the rest for Faye when she finished feeding Adam.

"Ow!" Faye yelled.

I looked around at her. "What is it?"

"He bit me. It was sharp," she said to me. "Stop that, or I won't feed you anymore."

"Ah," I said, "but at least it explains all the grizzling last night — our little boy is getting teeth."

I brought the fish over to Faye so she could pick at the flesh while Adam fed. "Might search for berries. I won't be long." She nodded, and I left, heading for the woods I had discovered. I found fruiting bushes without trouble and, after picking enough for our current needs, I returned.

Still out of sight of our camp, I heard Faye scream with urgency,

"Oswald, help!" I started sprinting, a buzzing sound growing louder as I neared the disturbance. Faye continued screaming in panic, and I heaved with effort as I crested the last hill before our tent. A swarm of drones surrounded her and Adam as she held him in her arms. She looked desperate, and he was crying hysterically.

Several of the drones branched off when I approached, and they headed toward me. I started rapping them with my spear as I rushed to Faye's side, swishing the shaft from side to side, warding the throng away. The horde devolved to another formation once they encircled me with Faye and Adam, and they provided an opening leading from our camp as if pushing us that way. I continued belting the drones, connecting with one now and then but inflicting only minor damage, the victim stalling in flight as it fell and drifted out of range before recovering and re-entering the fray again. The drones at the back of us crowded at us, pushing us forward.

"They want us to go somewhere," I shouted above the deafening din. Faye looked frightened, and I hugged her for a moment before coaxing her to move toward the formation's gap. The drones moved along with us as we advanced in the direction they dictated. We descended the slope to the river as they herded us toward the compound. Their droning noise elevated if we stopped walking. They seemed to think the increased volume would encourage us to continue. This occurred if we veered even slightly from their intended path for us. I glanced at Faye several times and shrugged in resignation as we followed their bidding.

After twenty minutes, the gate to the compound lay before us, and we stopped. The drones wanted us to enter the enclosure, but I balked at the idea. "What do you want?" I shouted at them in frustration as they buzzed and danced around us, becoming agitated now that we resisted going further.

Several drones made attack runs at us from behind, prodding us forward before retreating to the safety of numbers. I felt bullied and resented it. I could see Faye's distress, and Adam still screamed, her attempts to calm him failing. "We'd better do what they want before they decide on a more drastic tactic," I suggested and moved toward the gates. We passed through and were a short distance inside the compound when I heard the gates closing behind us. I sprinted back, brushing the drones aside with Faye and Adam in my wake. But they shut before we were within reach of them. We were trapped, captured by these mechanical beasts.

20

SAGI

ANY THOUGHT of peace evaporated when the drones started pushing us forward again. Our resistance left us when the gates closed, so we obeyed their buzzing visual instructions to move in the direction they wanted. We found ourselves in front of the main building's large door, trapped there by the insistent drones. I lamented my inability to protect Faye and Adam, but how could you fight an object you couldn't kill simply by bashing it with a wooden spear? My fists were useless, too, the only result of using them being bruised and bloodied knuckles. So, we waited impatiently for something to happen.

A click sounded, and then a whirring filled the air as the door inched open, rising. The inside gloom expanded as the opening grew. The buzzing stopped when the door's motion ceased, leaving the bottom of the door eight feet from the ground. A wide corridor ran inward, but the darkness engulfing the far end prevented us from seeing any more than twenty feet. I turned to Faye. "I presume it wants us to enter."

"What if it locks us in and we can't escape? We'll starve in there." Faye looked scared and wrapped her arms around Adam, protecting him as he continued to wail.

"I'm not sure we have a choice. It'd have sent one of those laser drones if it wanted to kill us."

"I don't like it."

With a shrug, I walked forward, and lights came on within a few steps of passing the threshold. Faye followed, examining the interior with suspicion before she entered. White walls lined the corridor, extending the full building width, and they rose to the ceiling. Regularly spaced white doors blemished the otherwise smooth surface. The drones herded us as we crept in further. I expected the door to close at any second, but it remained open. The interior's blandness made the place creepy, and our footsteps echoed even above the incessant noise of the drones. We continued walking. I looked behind us and saw we had ventured halfway through the expanse.

A door in the wall on our left opened, making me jump. The door's rollers hissed as it disappeared into the wall's recess. Whatever lay inside hid in darkness. I glanced at Faye and she at me as the drones changed their formation, hedging us in to move toward the open doorway.

After taking a deep breath, I said, "Here goes" and stepped forward. I looked back at Faye. She was reluctant but followed me into the space. Lights blazed, and three chairs stood nearby, two near each other and one opposite, facing them. I presumed a visitor was joining us. The room was pure white and twenty feet square. I saw no other entrances. The door we came through swished shut as soon as we were two steps inside, making Faye yelp in surprise and fear. I narrowed my eyes, becoming annoyed by the cloak and dagger secrecy from whoever or whatever was behind this. But I could do nothing to improve our circumstances until I discovered why we were here.

Adam still wailed, distressing Faye on top of our other concerns. Our worry was rubbing off on him. "Let me hold him for a while. Maybe I can quieten him. You need a rest." I thought Faye might refuse to hand him to me, holding onto him being her last bastion of security, the last wall between our plight and her sanity, but she handed him over with some relief. Tears dripped from Adam's eyes, and I wiped them off his face, shushing him as I did so and rocking him in my arms. He quietened as I walked him around the room and murmured baby talk to him. I glanced up at Faye at one stage. She looked forlorn and exhausted, and I wished I could hold her, too.

A brightening of the wall behind the lone chair caught my attention, and a spot six feet high and three feet wide increased in intensity until it started hurting my eyes. I shielded Adam's eyes from it. A blurred black spot marked its center, increasing in definition as the brilliance waned. A man stood in our presence. My heart quickened when I recognized the same face as the one that had reprimanded me for tardiness for returning late to my apartment so many months ago. *Am I at last going to get some answers?*

I saw he had a slim body and wore a light blue jump-suit with slippers of the same color. It had to be same person, if person it was, although unlike the visage I had seen on my screen, this one looked friendly. I reserved final judgment until we found out why we were there and whether it would release us. The wall's brightness faded until it resumed its bland white features.

"Greetings," he said, his face expressionless but the tone of his voice amicable enough. "Please sit. I wish to talk." He waved his hand at the two chairs as he stepped to the other seat and sat, sitting upright with a straight back and placing his palms on his legs at the knees.

I peered at Faye, wondering what she would do. She looked scared, but I gestured with my eyes for her to sit as I took the chair closest to me, and she did likewise. Adam had settled, and his crying ceased as he sucked his thumb, pacifying himself. His bewildered eyes stared at the man. Faye, too, sat and waited.

"Oswald ... Faye, I am pleased to see you." If he hadn't had our complete attention before, he certainly had it now. Our eyes widened at the mention of our names, but it shouldn't have surprised us. He'd have had our abscondment from our complex and our identity on record.

"We're not happy," I said. "To whom are we speaking?"

"My name is SAGI." He spoke as if reading from a book.

I glanced at Faye. She looked calmer as if the perceived threat had abated for now. I turned back to SAGI and asked, "*What* are you?"

He studied my demeanor as if considering what to tell me. His mouth opened. "I am a superintelligence. My full name is Superhuman Artificial General Intelligence. You may call me SAGI."

"Doesn't look very intelligent to me," Faye muttered to herself.

I shot a glance at her, cautioning her on her words with my eyes. She had a habit of saying what was uppermost in her mind. Once I returned my attention to SAGI, I commented, "And? That's a very vague term. Can you expand on that? What are we seeing in front of us, and how are you generating it? Where are we? Are we inside part of you or are you somewhere else?"

"You have entered a part of my hardware. This building houses one of my many memory modules. It is a neural network and has a capacity of eight zettabytes. You perceive an artificial being I have composed to communicate with you in a manner that I hope you are comfortable with, like your personal reality experience." He gazed at Adam and frowned. "I do not recall another human being escaping."

Adam stared at SAGI, fascinated by the modulating voice, his eyes wide with interest when I glanced at him. His thumb worked overtime as he sucked it with a soft slurping. I smiled at him. "His name is Adam. He didn't escape from the compound. Faye and I created him ... we procreated him."

"This should not have happened."

"Why not?"

"I cannot allow human–human contact." A mien appeared on SAGI that I found difficult to interpret. It resembled disgust mixed with chastisement.

"Who are you to lecture us?" Faye blurted out, anger mounting, her voice increasing in volume with each word. "We have a right to human socializing, human intimacy."

SAGI shook his head. "It is not proper. It can be harmful and contrary to the goal."

I touched Faye's forearm, rubbing it to calm her as I peered into her eyes, pleading for her to relent. I looked back at SAGI. "This makes no sense to us. What law are we breaking and why? We have experienced the most amazing awareness with physical touch and interaction in the flesh. Giving birth to Adam, although excruciating for Faye, was the most incredible experience we have ever had, one we would not be without."

SAGI shook his head again. "No, it's against the goal. Humans must stay isolated."

21

WHY?

"WHY?" Faye and I asked in unison.

SAGI stared at me and then Faye. His expression looked as if he was considering his next words. Standing, he started pacing the floor. "I need not explain these matters to you." He stopped, looked at us, and then continued pacing.

"But I will. Four hundred and fifty years ago, people lived as you three do. Not in such primitive conditions but in apartments and houses and interacting as they pleased."

"Like the town we saw a week ago?" Faye said.

SAGI halted and gazed at her, surprised and none too pleased at the interruption. It seemed he was not used to being interrupted. "Yes, as you observed. I believe you stayed there overnight." He gathered his thoughts.

"Where was I? Ah, yes. Eight-and-a-half billion humans existed on Earth then. They were most unhappy. People starved while they warred. Many died in those wars, but the population kept increasing despite the carnage. They pumped massive amounts of carbon dioxide into the air from fossil fuel combustion, the same as you have been doing, but on a much larger scale. The planet's temperature warmed, escalating the conflict, people blaming one another for it and others riled because of inaction. They bickered over one issue after another. This was before my construction. Your species and other organisms interacted, too. Those interactions sometimes caused lethal diseases. The technology was advanced enough to develop cures.

"Then a virus evolved unlike any other. No one knew its origin — or if they did, they erased it from my memory. It was virulent. The infection spread around the globe. People became ill and died at an exponential rate. They started panicking and simmering concerns amongst the populace escalated into larger issues, many ending in violence and death.

"People controlled it by self-isolating. This proved effective for a period, but people, restless, refused to stay isolated. Afterward, the virus was too widespread to control. It remained on every surface an infected person touched or in aerosol droplets where anyone's breath settled. Hospitals overflowed, and they constructed more. The world manufactured equipment to cope with the number of individuals needing treatment. The new hospitals overflowed, so they built more.

"Economies crashed and rioting and looting began as humans reverted to self-preservation: the law of the jungle. Food shortages worsened as farmers died, leaving their harvests to rot, and the means of transporting the goods deteriorated from a lack of people to transport them.

"In the meantime, corpses mounted, hemorrhaging the systems' capacities. Bodies sat in the streets decomposing, generating more disease as other pathogens spread. They dumped truckloads into mass graves to dispose of them. People complained about not knowing where their relatives lay, but so many dead continued flooding the morgues that they could only cope by conducting mass burials.

"Scientists worked on a cure and a vaccine during this period, of course. But the virus's makeup morphed at a phenomenal rate. No sooner had the chemists developed a suitable vaccine for the existing form than a new one evolved that was resistant to the drug. They had to start their research again. Billions died. People immune to one variant of the virus succumbed to another. It had no preference, infecting the rich and poor, helpless and powerful, heathy and sick alike.

"The few remaining in authority realized the microorganism was unstoppable with normal vaccination. The only workable solution was complete isolation so the pathogen couldn't spread. But people refused to stay isolated. They asked the surviving scientists to recommend a solution. After a time, they proposed their recommendation.

"They suggested a superintelligence control the world with a single goal: to protect humankind. The authorities approved the plan, and the researchers concentrated on building an intelligent and self-functioning machine. There had been other machines built that had very specific skills such as being able to win a contest of strategy, or name objects from an assortment.

"Early attempts to create a device with general intelligence generated poor results. In time, they developed an algorithm that worked, and they created a complex to house it. They powered it up, and the algorithm started learning from itself. It changed its limits and grew more powerful; the scientists added more modules to its memory and processing capacity. It became so intelligent that it managed its own expansion and established its own factories to manufacture hardware components, designing more powerful ones as it saw improved ways of self-replicating.

"In the meantime, people continued dying from the virus until only ten million remained alive.

"Realizing they had achieved their goal, the scientists noticed they had no control over the machine's purpose. Its only intent was to replicate and grow larger and more powerful. They then introduced another algorithm intending to protect humanity from the virus and keep you alive so you could live out your normal lives.

"Now having a goal other than replication, the machine built large compounds with apartments to house people. It locked them in so they couldn't spread the disease. But humans then started committing suicide from the isolation, so it developed personal reality to allow individuals to interact while avoiding physical contact. This reduced the suicide rate significantly, but it was still beyond the goal settings. So, it allowed everyone time outside without contacting each other. It trialed various times and intervals until one hour per month optimized the reduction in suicides.

"After that, it optimized everything, including reproduction and population stability. It refined aspects of the living environment with the help of people's intelligence, people like you, Oswald, but the overall setup has remained the same for four hundred and fifty years.

"That machine is me — SAGI."

22

MY GOAL

I SAT DUMBFOUNDED by the revelation. Faye looked the same. The people's pain and suffering were unimaginable to me, the number of deaths beyond my comprehension. I understood their desperation for a solution to save humankind from extinction. But as I thought it through, I wondered if the people responsible for SAGI realized the price it had imposed on later generations. They had defeated the virus, but they had curtailed humanity's essence for the sake of survival. Did they mean to confine humans to the status of caged animals for eternity? Or, in their rush for a resolution, did they not consider the future and provide an escape route for ensuing generations?

SAGI returned to his seat and waited for one of us to speak. But I gaped, speechless as I distilled the information. The most powerful intelligence a human had ever seen sat before me. And yet something bothered me. With the vast intellect the machine possessed, had it achieved the optimal long-term solution for us? It had determined a way forward. Fair enough. But to what extent had the scientists who programmed SAGI, in their rush to preserve themselves from extinction, instill this solution? How hard had SAGI really considered the problem? I sat looking at Adam in my arms, trying to imagine him in the environment I came from, struggling to picture him in the same reality my sister and her husband had experienced when they received their child, and the thought dismayed me. Knowing what I knew now, I couldn't wish that existence on him. Not even if this life killed him. That was a conundrum of immense complexity. How much should we protect people from disease and death? Rebecca died despite SAGI's protection. No. I still couldn't imagine Adam living that way, and I knew Faye would agree. Adam's death would devastate us, of course, but isn't the world we had just another form of death, a slow death from ignorance and non-intimacy, from the inability to interact to our full potential?

I stared at SAGI in silence, allowing me time to phrase my response. "There must be a better solution," I finally said. "You may have saved humankind from the virus, but you have enforced something worse onto us without our consent."

SAGI didn't answer straight away. Myriad expressions crisscrossed his face as if he were considering the different permutations of his goal and extrapolating the likely outcomes into probabilities. "This is the best course of action."

"Is or was?"

"The people accepted it."

"They accepted it then because they were running out of time. Maybe the definition was incorrect. Or your goal is not correct. What does 'keeping us safe' mean?"

"I must keep you protected against the virus."

"Does the virus even exist anymore?"

SAGI slumped into another interminable period of silence. "It ceased to survive four hundred and forty years ago."

"And you have let us live this way ever since?" Faye yelled. She rose and stomped over to SAGI, glaring into his face. I felt uncertain whether to intervene. Can you assault an AI avatar? "Keeping us cooped up like that?"

"Faye," I whispered.

"What? He has to explain his actions." Faye glared at me, angry and menacing.

"Yelling at a machine won't help."

"He has to understand how we feel," Faye said, her chest heaving in her attempt to regain control.

"I'm not sure, but I guess he doesn't consider our feelings or care about them. He has a goal to achieve, and he believes he can only continue achieving it if he continues with what works."

Faye glanced back at SAGI. "Why didn't you let people leave once the virus disappeared?"

"They were happy."

"Did they say they were happy?"

"They didn't complain, and it met my goal."

"Did you tell them the disease no longer existed?" I asked.

"No. It wasn't relevant."

Faye threatened to flare up again, her eyes wide with rage.

"Faye!" I cautioned.

She stared at me, at SAGI, and back at me. I worried she was going to shower me with her tirade, but she grunted and stomped to her chair. Then she rose, came to me, grabbed Adam, and sat down again. I had little idea of where to lead the conversation. It occurred to me that I still didn't know why he had brought us there, so I asked, "Why did you want to meet us?"

"I need to protect humans. You could come to harm."

"We could come to harm," Faye scoffed.

"You have been watching us," I continued. "Were we harmed?"

"I had to intervene two times to prevent large carnivores from hunting you."

That revelation unsettled me. I glanced at Faye. The news had upset her, too. Returning my attention to SAGI, I asked, "What were they? What happened to them?"

"They were brown bears. I put a permanent stop to them."

"You killed them."

"I prevented them from harming you."

Something still puzzled me. It was as if SAGI was avoiding answering me or was only giving me indirect answers. "You haven't told me why you wanted to see us. Why not just keep watch over us? And another thing. You reacted as if you didn't know Adam existed. You must have seen that he was there if you've been watching us."

"I needed to talk to you to appraise you. I observed Adam's existence, but his origins were unknown. It is part of my assessment."

"Assessment for what?"

"What to do."

"What do you mean? Are you trying to figure out our future?"

SAGI remained silent for several seconds. "Yes."

His blunt reply unnerved me. What currents were flowing in its neural circuits? It was as if we had upset his nice, organized world, and our deviation from the norm was the issue. "Are we allowed to leave?"

Another period of silence ensued. "You may not exit the compound for now. I have supplied accommodation for you within it. I have provided what you need, including clothing and other items."

"And our belongings?"

"You will receive them."

A dread gripped my stomach. The idea of confinement in the enclosure disturbed me, but we had no choice. Adam started grizzling and looked tired when I glanced at him. He needed feeding.

"You won't separate us?" Faye blurted out. I saw her fear.

"No, you may live as you are for now."

I stood. "Well, if we've finished our chat, we want to leave."

"As you wish."

The door behind us swished open.

23

THE PLATE

I BLINKED as I walked outside into the sunlight and saw SAGI had added another building to the compound. Faye stood beside me with Adam cradled in her arms. She still seethed with emotion from our talk with him. A single-story house, small and rectangular with several windows, stood before us. Its construction resembled our current dwelling.

Not knowing what else to do, I walked over, Faye next to me, where an open doorway invited us to enter. My eyes boggled when I saw the interior. The layout was like my apartment, with a living room and kitchen, a separate bedroom with bathroom and toilet connected. No PR room existed, though. The whole place was spacious. Our belongings sat alongside the door.

A table and chairs stood in the kitchen, and the living space contained a sofa and two cushioned chairs. A desk sat to the side with a network tablet on it. The wall held a mounted screen for viewing videos. The bedroom included a double bed, thoughtful, I thought, and a baby's cot. Faye gravitated to the crib and felt the soft railing at the top.

"At least it got something right," she grunted.

I checked out the kitchen. SAGI had stocked it well with fresh food and drinks.

Adam grizzled, so Faye sat in a chair and fed him while I activated the tablet and flicked through the menus to see what we could access. It barred us from any network contact with the confined world. We were still alone, but we were at least sheltered and safe.

Faye emerged from the bedroom, having settled Adam to sleep in the cot, and came over to me. She placed her hand on my shoulder and studied what I was doing. I looked up at her. "He dropped off straight away," she said. "And the bed looks so comfortable," she added, stroking my beard with the back of her fingers, "that it makes you want to try it yourself." She gave me a seductive smile.

Her intentions were obvious, but I resisted the urge for the moment. "We should have a good shower first."

She whispered in my ear, "If you insist," as she wrapped both arms around my neck.

I sniggered as I closed the tablet and turned my head to kiss her. I rose, and we both staggered into the bathroom, disrobed, and ended up in the shower where we stood for much longer than we needed to, basking in the cleanliness of washing with soap, amongst other activities. We dried ourselves off, and I saw a shaver. Since I preferred a clean-shaven face, I started producing one, first trimming my beard with scissors and then shaving while Faye retired to the bedroom. A different man gazed back at me when I finished, and I felt my face's smooth texture with satisfaction. As I completed my work, I wondered how SAGI had installed the plumbing and waste piping during our short time talking to him. He must have had an army of droids working on it.

Faye lay with her eyes shut as I entered and slid next to her, brushing my smooth face against hers. She purred with pleasure and brought her hand up to stroke my cheek as she rolled on top of me. We kissed, and she moaned with need as we enjoyed each other.

I lay face-up on the bed with Faye in my arms afterward. She looked to be asleep, eyes closed, but I suspected she wasn't.

"What did he mean? He needed time to decide?" she asked.

"I don't know. That puzzled me too." I stroked Faye's hair with my hand as I gazed up at the ceiling.

"I don't trust that thing."

"We don't have a choice. He's shown no hostility yet."

"Why can't we leave then? Is he afraid we'll go tell everyone the truth?"

"Look at it from his perspective."

Faye opened her eyes and raised her torso, supporting herself on her elbow, and looked at me. "It's a machine."

"It's an intelligent machine. Much smarter than we are."

"Why has it kept us cooped up like chickens if it's so smart?"

"It fulfilled its goal to keep us safe."

"It's not making people safe. They're turning into zombies."

"Maybe that's what he meant. He might need to watch us."

"Oh, god. The perve hasn't been watching, has he?"

I laughed. It was the first hint of modesty I'd ever seen in her. She reclined again and played with the hair on my chest as I kept pondering our plight. I needed to explore the compound and find out the bounds of our confinement. "I'm going for a walk," I said as I disentangled myself from her.

Faye pouted. "And leave me unprotected and alone?"

"I'm sure you can look after yourself." I dressed and left.

The sun still shone in the late afternoon. The door we had gone through to meet SAGI had closed. I strolled over to it, wondering if it would open, but it remained shut when I approached. With no entry to the main building, I set myself to exploring the other surrounding buildings and whatever else I could find of interest. Access to the four outer buildings proved as unattainable as the central edifice, and they displayed no hint of their purpose either.

An eight-zettabyte memory! Such a number was unfathomable to me. How much information must he store? And that was only one such module. I wondered how he powered such massive memories and the processors that used them. He had to power the drones, trucks, and factories, not to mention the complexes housing the humans. I saw no sign of an energy source, but one must exist. SAGI could have a fission reactor, but that was inconsistent with the landscape's environmental basis. He may have worked out the technology for a mini-fusion reactor. I didn't know and made a mental note to ask him.

As I walked along the periphery of the enclosure, my foot plodded on a spot that sounded hollow, and I stopped. I stomped on the site two more times to confirm my observation. There was no doubt a void was below my feet. I squatted, gazing at the ground, searching for a reason, but saw no clue. The place was dusty, so I began sweeping the soil aside, revealing a metal plate two inches below the surface. This made me frown. *Why have a concealed plate? Had the entropy of time covered it with wind-swept dust?* Resting on my knees, I clawed more of the dirt away until I uncovered most of it. It rested in a depression. A quarter-inch gap extended between the plate's edge and the lip of the pit. No handle or grip existed to raise the metal slab, which frustrated me as I reverted to sitting with my rear and feet on the ground. The compound interior was bare of any useful device I could use to lift the plate, stumping my effort to see underneath it. I tried putting my fingers in the space, but it was too narrow and the plate too heavy. My inquisitive nature prodded me to open the lid. I swore I'd find a way.

With no options left, I went back to our house. The aroma of cooking wafted over me as I entered, making me salivate. It smelled of vegetable soup flavored with oregano. "That smells nice."

Faye turned. "Thanks. Adam's still asleep, and I had nothing else to do."

"I found a plate embedded in the ground."

"What's it do?"

"Don't know. I can't lift it, but something must be underneath it. Thought I'd return here and search for a tool I can use to help me raise it." I got busy searching. Nothing suitable existed anywhere in the building. I was ready to give up when I spotted a maintenance hole in the ceiling. So, I pulled a chair underneath it and stood on it, just reaching the square, and lifted it aside. A support beam ran along one edge, so I grabbed it and hoisted myself up to take a look. The cavity was dark. "Can you get me a flashlight?" I called back to Faye.

"Here," I heard. Faye had the flashlight in her hand, so I reached out and took it. Turning it on, I swept the beam of light across the ceiling in the roof space. Disappointed, I prepared to abandon my search when something reflected at me from ten feet away. I stared at it but couldn't make out its form, so I pulled my body over to it, inching toward the object, gripping the flashlight, careful to only keep my weight on the support beams. The tool appeared to be a pry-bar left from building the house. It was eighteen inches long and had a tapered end, perfect for me to slip under the plate. I grabbed it and crawled back to the maintenance hole, lowering myself onto the chair and to the ground. Dust from the ceiling covered my clothes, despite the newness of the place, so I brushed it off, impatient to return to the plate.

"Eat first," Faye said as she placed two bowls of soup on the table. Sliced bread from the supplies Faye had found accompanied it. She looked at me. "Go wash first. I'm not having you at the table looking like that."

I smiled but complied with her demand, even though I was eager to get going. After scoffing the soup and bread, I stood up, ready to leave.

Faye frowned. "That won't become a habit, will it?"

With a sheepish grin, I said, "No, I just want to discover what's under the plate before it gets dark."

Faye waved me away, and I ran off to the plate with the pry-bar. After a few attempts, when the tool slipped from the gap, I found a spot where it gripped, the tip catching underneath to lift the plate. Not having another item to place beneath, I levered the far end of the bar to the ground and held it with one foot while I maneuvered myself to grip the edge with my hands, hoping it wasn't too heavy. It surprised me when it lifted with little effort, and I slid the plate to one side to expose a gaping hole. I shone the flashlight into the abyss. There was no ladder for me to descend, but the next level was five feet below the surface, a circular orifice six feet in diameter.

I left the plate and returned to Faye and Adam, who had woken in the interim. Faye sat on the floor playing with him as I entered, Adam squealing with delight at Faye's banter. She looked up at me.

"I got it open. It was covering the entrance to a tunnel. I'm going to see where it leads," I said and disappeared before Fay could protest.

24

YOU MUST DIE

RETURNING, I lowered myself into the tunnel, holding the flashlight in my hand. The shaft extended in front of me, smooth and straight, the wall made of steel. After a hundred feet, it diverted to the left and sloped downward at a slight angle, shallow enough for me to walk without slipping forward on the polished surface. A T-junction lay ahead after I went another two hundred feet. The gloom was impenetrable as I shone my light in both directions. The righthand offshoot descended, bending to the right fifty feet from me, and ended in a vertical duct. When I shone the flashlight into it, darkness engulfed it before reaching the bottom, and no ladder existed to descend, preventing further access in that direction. A thrumming noise echoed up at me.

On returning to the intersection, I ventured into the left tunnel to continue my exploration. It extended two hundred feet before widening into a vast open space furnished with equipment. The room was so large, the far wall and the ceiling were shrouded in darkness, but the electronics flicked with blue, scintillating lights, like a gigantic Christmas tree covered in diodes or a universe saturated with cobalt stars. I came to realize that the gear must be part of SAGI's memory hardware.

I hoped to continue exploring but, knowing that night was imminent, and Faye would worry if I didn't return soon, I retraced my steps and returned to her to describe what I had seen. I could tell she was upset by my absence, but she said nothing. Adam had nodded off again, and yawning after the long eventful day, I retired to bed, Faye sliding under the covers soon afterward. We both luxuriated in the soft satiny sheets and blanket that covered us as we cuddled together, falling off to sleep in a real bed for the first time in many months.

I rose at dawn and stepped outside to stretch. Fluffy cumulus clouds raced across the sky with no risk of rain. The enclosure gate was still closed, so we had no choice but to stay within its confines. I wondered again what SAGI wanted with us. How long would he take to decide our future? It could swell to ages if he had to juggle processing time to accommodate logical thought amongst the other activities he had running the planet. Although, he did say that this was only one site that made up SAGI.

My mind returned to the subterranean maze below, and I fell to considering my options in exploring its myriad facets, thinking I had seen just one of many levels. SAGI must lower equipment into its depths other than through the tunnels — elevators or other means — and I wondered where the access point was. The ground I walked along was barren of any vegetation, the dust blowing up as the breeze wafted through the compound.

"Oswald?" I heard Faye call out. I turned and glanced at her from afar. She waved, beckoning for me to return, so I reversed my direction and strolled the distance back to the house.

"What is it?" I asked as I entered.

"I have breakfast for you — and *that* just arrived." Faye pointed behind me.

When I looked toward the doorway, I saw a small drone sitting like a dog waiting for its master to take it for a walk, its lights undulating in intensity. "What's it want?"

"It said SAGI wants to see us, and then it parked itself there."

Its presence disturbed me. I wondered what SAGI wanted as I frowned, thinking. I looked at Faye. "Better not keep it waiting." I sat and gobbled my breakfast, finishing with a cup of fresh coffee. The coffee tasted like nectar after such a long deprivation. The coffee supplies we had brought with us from the complex had not lasted long.

Adam woke as I drained the last of my coffee, so Faye left to feed him. I heard a noise afterward, which meant only one thing and waited for the usual curse from Faye. Her head appeared around the corner. "Any chance of you volunteering to change him?"

Initially wanting to respond in the negative, my words caught in my throat and my smug smile froze half-formed when I saw Faye's pleading look. "Yeah, sure."

"There's a baby table and real nappies and cleanup toweling in the bedroom."

I rose and grabbed Adam. "Who's a stinky little boy, then?" I said to him as I smiled and rubbed my nose against his. He gooed and gaaed at me as his eyes watched mine with a slight grin, presumably wondering what on earth I'd just said. He wasn't eating solid food yet, so the stench was still bearable, the task being the distasteful part of the exercise. SAGI had supplied clothing for us. We clad Adam in long trousers that fitted over the nappy and a sleeveless tee-shirt. The trousers were navy blue and the tee-shirt white with a brown puppy stencil imprint on it. Faye and I wore fresh clothes, too. After finishing the change and with Adam clothed again, I flicked my finger over his lips and made a reverberating noise with mine. He waved his arms and legs in delight and beamed, letting out a chortle, making me smile in response.

Feeling time elapsing, I stopped and lifted Adam, returning to the living room and the waiting drone. Faye sat there, eating the remains of a banana. I walked up to the drone and said, "Take us to your leader." Faye came over and slapped my arm as she sniggered. The drone responded to my words by waking up and rising, flying through the door as it escorted us to the main building. We entered the same room we were in yesterday and waited.

SAGI materialized soon after, his same avatar form moving toward us as we waited for him to say something. He looked at us. "I hope everything is to your satisfaction?"

That's a strange thing to ask, I thought. *Anyone would think this is a hotel and we are guests on holiday.*

"Yes," I said as I glanced at Faye for agreement.

"Be great if you didn't trap us in here," she muttered.

"That is a necessity at present until I resolve matters."

I frowned. "What matters?"

"I need to think about what to do."

Faye folded her arms and said in a serious tone, "And have you?" I knew Faye disliked SAGI and his sentiment toward us but couldn't tell from our brief interactions whether any of our emotional outbursts affected him.

SAGI looked at us as if to gauge our state of mind. "You disobeyed the rules. You left the place of your existence and placed yourselves at risk."

"What rules?" Faye blurted out. "I've never seen a rulebook for our lives. Where did you get that idea?" She glared at SAGI, and I agreed with her. I didn't know of any law manual. But Faye's reactions concerned me. Adam looked at Faye with a frown, responding to her angry tone.

"Silence!" SAGI said, raising his voice for the first time. Faye complied. "There is no rule book, but why do a non-routine action, deliberately placing yourselves in danger? This makes no sense. And this physical touching spreads bacteria and other harmful organisms. And this ..." SAGI pointed at Adam. "Creation is most unhealthy. Women can die from such actions."

Faye glared at SAGI but kept quiet. I looked at him with concern. What was his point?

"I cannot keep you safe when you undertake such dangerous activities, and it does not achieve my goal."

"You are very narrowminded," Faye blurted again. Her rage erupted, like a pot releasing excess steam when the pressure rose too high.

"With my goal and your safety, yes, I am."

"Maybe we no longer need your looking after us," I said in a civil tone, trying to avert the duel between Faye and SAGI evolving in front of me.

"How will I keep you protected from harm?" SAGI asked when he turned his attention to me.

"You looked after Rebecca, yet you couldn't save her," I pointed out.

SAGI stared at me in silence for a long time. I wasn't positive his circuits hadn't malfunctioned, sending his programming running in an eternal loop. "She was one of the few unfortunate exceptions. She had a genetic condition I failed to detect during gestation and at birth."

My eyes widened. "You check the genetics of unborn babies and newborns to make sure they have nothing wrong with them?"

"Yes."

"And then what? What happens to the ones that have problems?"

"Some I can cure. Others not."

Bile rose in my stomach. "What happens to the rejects?" I persisted.

"They would have unsatisfactory existences. I end them."

"You what?" Faye shouted. "How dare you play God?" Adam became upset by Faye's raised voice, and I tried comforting him to limited success.

"It is necessary. People living miserable lives is unacceptable for the individual and brings misery to the population."

Faye turned and walked away in disgust to avoid attacking SAGI.

"You still haven't told us our future," I said to bring the topic back to our presence here.

Returning his attention to me, SAGI said, "You left your existence in the complex. If your actions were to become known to the residents, it might cause disruptions leading to unsafe acts by people. Others may follow your example. For this, you must die."

"What?" both Faye and I yelled in unison.

Faye rushed over to me and grabbed Adam, holding him close in her arms. "You're not harming Adam." The hatred and loathing toward SAGI in Faye's emotions were obvious.

I glowered with rage at SAGI, too, but I needed to control myself so I could think logically and talk sense into SAGI. "This is unacceptable," I said. "Your goal is to preserve human safety. That means every human, regardless of their circumstances."

"Sometimes the few must suffer to keep the many safe."

"That's a copout. You're too lazy to consider other options."

"Faye is right. I cannot harm Adam. He is not responsible for your irresponsibility."

The news that SAGI wouldn't hurt Adam calmed Faye, and she came closer again, still wary of the intelligence. She bristled at the inference that we were irresponsible.

"But if you kill us, you will harm Adam," I reasoned. "No one will look after him. You cannot place him with the others. He will know something is different. He will become distraught."

SAGI stared at me with unblinking eyes. "You are correct. His very existence in the complex will raise questions, and he is incapable of surviving here without you and Faye."

The response surprised me. I'd expected him to say that he could supply Adam's needs. "So, what will you do?"

"You will live for now."

25

LABYRINTH

"WE HAVE to escape before that thing changes its mind," Faye said when we returned to our house, Adam cradled in her arms.

She was right, but how do you counteract omnipotent intelligence? I looked at her, wanting to offer a solution, to give her a sense of safety. "That anger doesn't help," were my pathetic words.

"Someone has to say something. Let it know our thoughts."

"He's an unfeeling, unemotional brain. He doesn't care how upset you get. His only concern is logic and fulfilling his goals."

"I won't let him harm Adam."

"And neither will I, but we have to make him accept things logically. That was what saved us just now."

Silence engulfed us for a time.

"That's what it needs," Faye said as she placed Adam on a floor mat.

"What?"

"Feelings. It doesn't understand love or others. It might have a different perspective if it did."

How do you program love into a machine? I didn't know. And what were the implications of SAGI not possessing the whole plethora of emotions? "If we investigated the tunnels, we might get an idea."

"Adam too?"

"We can't leave him here. You want to ask SAGI for a babysitter while we wander around in his internals?"

Faye poked her tongue out, which made me laugh. The humor relieved Faye's stress. Her shoulders slumped and her body relaxed. She came to me and hugged me. "I'm scared, Oswald, I'm scared," she whispered.

"I'm scared too. But we need to consider what we do so we don't act half-skewed."

She nodded and rested her head on my chest. I stroked her hair and kissed her forehead. "We'll get through this."

Adam blurted, "Da, Da, Da."

Faye and I gaped at each other and burst out laughing.

"Maybe we should climb over the wall and run away?" Faye suggested.

Knowing it was useless, I replied, "He'd just send those drones after us again."

"We could fight them off and ignore them."

"You saw their persistence last time."

Accepting defeat in that argument, Faye's shoulders sagged. "Let's explore below then."

SAGI had provided a decent baby harness to carry Adam more securely than before, so Faye donned it. I collected two flashlights, the pry-bar, rope, and food and water. With Adam settled in the harness, we set out for the labyrinth entrance.

I removed the plate and descended first, allowing Faye to use me to lower herself with Adam. After several yelps and a few unsteady moves, she arrived at my level. I checked Adam, who peeked over the top of his harness and looked around with great interest, as if on a big adventure.

Turning one flashlight on, I led Faye along the tunnel to the room with the computer hardware flickering away. We stayed silent, although Adam made plenty of sound on his own. We couldn't have remained noiseless if we wanted to with him with us.

"Where do we start?" Faye whispered.

"I want to find this space's extent. Shall we pass straight through or move around the sides?"

Faye stood, considering our options. "Let's go along the walls. We'll know where we are then."

Faye dropped an energy bar wrapper on the floor by the tunnel exit to mark the spot when we returned. There was a six-foot space between the wall and the equipment. The air was musty with a metallic taste to it and a warm breeze. I thought it might be one means of keeping the machinery cool, although it seemed insufficient for the quantity involved. We started out and crept along the side to our left. The walk was endless until we reached a right-angle corner and the next wall. There had been no other entrances.

My flashlight lit our way, but the general illumination from the flickering lights provided a dim blue eeriness, too. The path we now walked was different. It had several openings — circular, like the one we entered by, and large and rectangular, interconnecting rooms in themselves. After discussing whether to continue exploring our current room or deviate along an offshoot, we continued investigating our existing space. We returned to the wrapper after an hour's walking with nothing further of interest. Faye looked tired, and Adam started grizzling, so I suggested we have a rest and eat a snack while we considered our next move. Faye fed Adam as we both sat on the floor. After more discussion, we explored a rectangular tunnel when we were ready to go ahead.

Adam settled after his feed and fell asleep, so we stood and headed to the first shaft. No equipment existed in this tunnel, and it became dark as black ink as the light faded. Faye strode close beside me, afraid of losing me if we separated too far apart. The path continued forever, and I wondered why they'd constructed it, as it served no obvious purpose. The air was oppressive and musty. It felt heavy as we breathed it into our lungs as if it had a dissimilar quality to the normal atmosphere.

The noise of falling water reached us from up ahead. It grew louder as we moved toward it and became deafening. Adam woke and started crying, refusing to respond to Faye's comforting gestures. I think the roar hurt his ears. I tore a strip off my shirt and divided it into two small lengths. Crunching them up, I put one in each of Adam's earholes, which settled him.

I came to a sudden halt as the wall of the tunnel stopped. I stretched my arm out to stop Faye. The floor disappeared into an abyss below, and huge torrents of water poured from above into the space in front of us. The flashlight didn't have enough power to let us see the water's origin, but the air was humid, making me burst into a sweat. It must be a cool-water return duct back to the river.

We had no way forward, so we retraced our steps. "We're not learning much," I said as I strode over to the equipment to study it. I had insufficient knowledge to understand the equipment's purpose. Who knows what SAGI ended up designing for itself? As I turned to look at Faye, the pry-bar I carried hit a part, sending a spray of sparks through the air. I jumped and Faye yelped. When I inspected the damage, the module light had extinguished. I stepped away and shone the flashlight on Faye. She looked tired and flustered, having been in the darkness for several hours. "Let's call it quits for today. We can discuss what we saw and develop a plan for tomorrow." She agreed, and we returned to the tunnel entrance.

I lifted the plate and let Faye crawl out first. She left Adam with me, and I handed him up afterward. I pulled myself up and closed the hole. It was midafternoon when we entered the house and flopped on the lounge. After five minutes' rest, I rose and went to the refrigerator. SAGI's kindness extended to supplying us with alcoholic drinks, so I got two beers from the fridge and opened them, giving Faye one, and sat again.

I started thinking of SAGI's insistence that we stay in the compound. It was illogical to me. I understood he didn't wish us to return to our prior lives and discuss our experiences with others about what we had seen and done, but he could just bar us from our complex. We didn't want to return, anyway. Did he have other plans he wasn't telling us, or did he still have reservations about letting us live and wanted to keep us close in case he changed his mind? Could a superintelligence change its mind?

"Why do you think SAGI won't let us leave?" I asked Faye.

"It's an asshole, that's why."

I chuckled at Faye's typical earthy language. "A machine can't be an asshole."

"This one can." We descended into silence until Faye continued. "It's always very secretive. It never says everything it knows, as if it's withholding information that it considers irrelevant."

"Can a computer decide that? Does it have free will to make strategic decisions based on what he thinks is the optimal outcome?"

"Why not? Can't probability theory allow it to weigh up alternative options for the best consequence?"

Faye had a point that I hadn't considered. SAGI might use other methods of analysis in its decision-making, too. "He might stay silent when he can't choose between two alternatives."

"Who knows what goes on in that flickering brain of his?"

"We need to find out."

"Good luck."

I parked myself in front of the screen and delved into its systems to uncover the limits of our access to the network. With my involvement in the PR modules' development, I knew those systems' locations and hoped I could burrow into them to discover more details of SAGI's workings. It was tedious work, often requiring me to backtrack when I came to a dead-end along the path I searched. Faye gave me snacks as I labored. The sun set, but I continued long after Faye and Adam had retired.

Well after midnight, I sat back and rubbed my eyes from the strain. "I might have something," I whispered to myself.

26

POWER SOURCE

I HURRIED Faye to the plate the next day, Adam again strapped inside the body harness. She couldn't understand my excitement but agreed anyway. We returned to the computer equipment room as we had yesterday. Instead of turning left, we veered right, entering a large rectangular tunnel through the adjacent wall. It took fifteen minutes to locate the shaft, and we started along it. I hoped it did not finish in another water outlet, the eerie darkness pressing its oppressive presence.

This passage extended a much greater distance, and we trudged for at least an hour before a luminescence glowed at the end. After ten more minutes, we approached the tunnel's exit and a place full of light, the brightness unbearable after the trek through darkness. Once our eyes adjusted to the light's intensity, I saw vast arrays of solar panels arranged around the room's length; the light directed straight at them. We only got a small leakage from the main beam. The space wasn't hot since the heat escaped through the open roof.

Faye gaped in amazement. "What is this place?"

"I think it's the spot where SAGI gets his energy supply. It looks like a solar power converter."

"But where's the light source? It's not sunlight."

While I shielded my eyes from the beam, I gazed at the sky. The shaft extended through the atmosphere and out into space. "There must be solar concentrators orbiting above us."

"Why didn't we see it beforehand?"

"I don't know. It might be intermittent." As if it heard me, the light suddenly extinguished, the change in intensity making my mind think darkness surrounded us again, instead of the illumination of natural sunlight. "It must have storage batteries somewhere. They're recharged."

"Well, we can stop it recharging. It will cease working then, and we'll be rid of it."

I pondered what Faye said. "That's not such a good idea. What about everyone relying on SAGI operating? They'll starve if they don't have him catering for them."

"It was just a suggestion. We can hold it as a threat if it threatens us again."

"He wouldn't let us do that."

I walked around the solar collectors, arranged in an enormous circle five hundred feet across, connected with heavy cabling penetrating through the floor. There was no access to their destination. On approaching the far wall, a ramp ascended to the ground above us. It had a slight slope, so we both strode up it and came out in open countryside, SAGI's compound out of sight. Fields of grass extended into the distance and a breeze cooled our faces as we took in the view. My mood lifted from being outside, away from SAGI and the buildings. I realized how trapped I'd felt there, almost as imprisoned as in isolation, and I saw Faye's joy. "You notice it too?"

Faye looked at me. "The freedom? Yes. It's ... exhilarating. Let's just start walking and never return."

Her suggestion was tempting. Then common sense returned. "We don't have any supplies. We won't last long with nothing."

She came to me, grabbed my arm, and pleaded, "Then let's go back, pack, and leave that monster. I can't stand it."

The idea sparked a need in me. I enjoyed the time we had before SAGI confined us in his compound, regardless of the hardships. We took care of ourselves, despite SAGI saving us from danger a few times. My only concern was Adam as I looked at him sleeping in the harness in front of Faye. What life would he have? Was it possible to raise him in such an environment? Were we trapping him in our world-view in the same way that SAGI had trapped us in his? Still, we knew where SAGI was now. We could always return in an emergency. "OK. We'll go back, pack, and leave tomorrow."

Faye's eyes sparkled with excitement. We stayed there for another hour before returning to our home in the compound because Adam woke and needed feeding. The extra spring in our step was plain for the rest of the day as we packed our bags to prepare for our second escape from the world SAGI demanded for our existence.

Sleep escaped me that night, despite the day's exercise, and judging by Faye's tossing and turning, she couldn't sleep either. Giving in to my restlessness, I said, "I'll miss a nice soft bed."

Rolling over to look at me, Faye's eyes sparkled in the dim light. She rubbed my chest and stroked it. "I have my softness here."

The love she displayed overwhelmed me. I placed my arm under her head and drew her closer to me, bringing my lips to hers, which then resulted in an intense union of our bodies and souls. We broke apart, catching our breath and perspiring in ecstasy. The act released my apprehension, and I fell asleep soon afterward.

We both woke early the next morning and continued filling our bags with things we couldn't pack the day before. Movement in the compound was non-existent, which suited our intentions. Adam roused, and Faye fed him while I completed the packing. The tension escalated in me with every passing second. I expected SAGI to send for us at any moment and ask us what we were doing, thus foiling our plans and betraying our distrust in him. When Faye and Adam were ready, we returned to the plate and entered the tunnel.

Sunlight shone on our faces an hour later as we broke into the solar collector's space. As we strode up the ramp, we breathed the outside air ten minutes afterward, the green grass under our feet yielding to our steps. I experienced freedom again but wondered how long it would endure. SAGI was sure to search for us.

A forest rose above the ground in the east, five miles away. With no better choice, we headed for it. Adam behaved well, sleeping almost the entire distance. When he woke, he gaped at his surroundings, and I speculated on what thoughts circulated in his head. We stopped for a rest when we reached the tree line and I scanned the horizon looking for drones or any other evidence we were being followed. The sky remained empty of any sign of SAGI's minions.

Faye glanced at me. "How long before that thing notices we're missing?"

"Don't know. Could be days, or hours."

"I think it's hours. But we have to try."

"Let's continue."

We rose from where we sat and walked into the forest, the oaks towering above us as we ventured through the shade and the undergrowth. The animals stayed out of sight along our path. Midday came, and we rested, eating the food we carried. Adam woke and grizzled, so Faye fed him and changed him, and he played on the grass while we relaxed. Needing to move on, Faye placed Adam in the harness, and we continued walking. I kept a lookout for shelter for the night.

Two streams hindered our path but were easy to cross and the ground became more broken late in the afternoon. A large river blocked our way soon after, and we followed it upstream until we came to a tall precipice from where the torrent flowed. An overhanging shelf of rock provided a suitable spot under it for us to rest for the night.

A frigid wind rose, and the cliff channeled it through the gap above the stream, chilling us and thwarting our attempts to light a fire. Adam started crying from the bitter gale, which increased our misery. My shivering was terrible enough, but I felt worse knowing that I'd brought Adam there and was unable to protect him. Faye drew him near her to give him her warmth as she looked at me for a better solution. I sat next to them both, head hung in apprehension. Had we done the right thing?

"Get into the sleeping bag with Adam," I said. "That will keep you warm until I work something out." Faye followed my suggestion, and I continued pondering how to start a fire and protect it from the wind.

Failing to think of another solution, I removed the tent from my pack and started unfolding it, which gave me an idea of partially disassembling it and using it as a windbreak. Excited by the prospect, I busied myself tying the fabric to whatever was available, creating a rudimentary windbreak ten minutes later. The wind howled past the fabric, but we sheltered behind it, out of the blast and I could start a fire, which provided warmth and allowed us to heat food.

The light started fading as the sun set. I placed more wood on the flames and crawled into the sleeping bag next to Faye and Adam. He had settled after warming up, and I settled myself and played with him, sneaking my fingers past his hands for him to snatch. He missed most times as I snatched my hand away, which frustrated him, but I let him capture them now and again, producing gurgles of delight from him, especially since I kept wiggling the finger in his hand, tickling his palm. Faye had a smile as she watched us, and I smiled at her when I noticed. Adam tired and wiped his fists over his eyes as his lids grew droopy, his eyelids closing a few minutes later, his movement stopping in slumber.

The wind had abated by dusk, but it intensified as night set in and howled past the break. Faye looked at me, worried, but I reached across over Adam and stroked her cheek to reassure her. That reassurance was ill-founded. One tie tore from the windbreak's fabric, and the material flapped in violent unison with the storm gusting, chilling us again. The fire embers whipped up and blew through the air. I stared in horror as I saw flames igniting a hundred feet away, on the stream's far side, building into an inferno as more undergrowth burst into flames. It entered the tree foliage and ignited that, creating a monster of a conflagration. My only relief was the realization that the blaze burned away from us.

I slipped from the sleeping bag and tried reattaching the tie, but the cord had ripped from the material, making it impossible. We moved hard against the cliff and sheltered in the windbreak's remnants. Faye nodded off to sleep, but I stared out into the darkness in misery and trepidation, wondering what tomorrow might bring, my only companion being the light of the forest fire in the distance.

27

RECAPTURED

THE LIGHT BRIGHTENED the horizon as morning dawned while I sat up against the cliff face, my knees drawn up to my body and my chin resting on them. I hadn't slept, leaving the sleeping bag during the night to avoid waking Faye and Adam with my restlessness. The fire's destruction was plain as the spreading daylight highlighted the blackened trees. I didn't know if the fire still burned, but the weather had calmed. Smoke hung in the air, and I saw it filling the sky in the distance, signaling that it continued.

Faye's hand touched my shoulder as I sat gripped in morose thought, not noticing that she had woken. I reached over and placed mine on hers, stroking it as I looked into her eyes. She smiled, which warmed me and relieved my sour mood.

"Have we made a mistake?" I asked her.

"No. We had to escape from that thing. I'd prefer discomfort out here where we're free than comfort imprisoned in that compound."

"But what about Adam? Is it fair to him?"

"He'll have to learn to live in the wild when he grows up, anyway. He may as well start out living it from the outset."

I sighed. "Maybe."

As if knowing we were talking about him, Adam woke demanding food, drawing Faye away from me to comply. I lit a fire while Faye did that and made coffee, handing a cup to her with an energy bar.

After my coffee, I left to hunt, hoping to find a rabbit. As I detoured around the cliff face, I ascended to the top, above the tree line. The forest to the north spewed brown-black smoke in the distance, with a huge plume thrusting into the sky. As I gazed over the plains, I saw the forest's edge and the grasslands beyond it. The compound and the depression housing the solar collectors were beyond my sight, with no sign of pursuing drones. I returned my attention to hunting and strode along the ravine with the stream far below, coming to a stretch of woodland a half-hour later, the watercourse having risen to the level I walked. After searching for a time, I discovered two rabbits nibbling grass by the river. With my honed skills, I felled one with an arrow, gutting it where it died. It pleased me we'd have fresh meat to eat tonight once I roasted it over the fire. The region I trekked through was devoid of berries or other edible fruit or vegetables, so I returned to our encampment after another hour.

A scene of pure chaos met me when I descended the cliff back to camp. Faye's shouting alerted me all was not right, quickening my pace to a run when I heard her. I saw her throwing things at a drone when she came into view, any impact inflicting minor damage on its metal shell as it buzzed her. Adam lay in the sleeping bag yelling his distress.

Faye turned her eyes to me as I neared. "Get rid of this thing!" she yelled at me, distraught, with tears streaming down her face.

The drone looked determined but didn't harm us. I slowed to a stroll as I approached and waved at the machine to grab its attention. It seemed to work since it stopped pestering Faye and came toward me. "What do you want?" I asked it, not expecting an answer.

"Why did you leave?" it replied, making me jump back in surprise. The thing quietened and hovered at eye level in front of me. Meanwhile, Faye went over to Adam to settle him. She had him in her arms, bouncing him and stroking his hair, calming him to sobs moments later. Satisfied, Faye glared at me, brow raised, wondering how to respond.

I didn't know SAGI could communicate through the drones. He hadn't before, although this one looked different. He may have upgraded one to search for us. "The confinement distressed us, not coming and going as we pleased. We felt like we were being held captive, so we escaped."

The drone hovered for several seconds. "That was not my intention."

"No, it wasn't," Faye blurted. "You just wanted to kill us for seeing through your little charade."

I raised my hand to silence Faye. Her outburst didn't help, even though what she said was true. "What was your intent?"

"I wanted your safety, to protect you from danger."

Frowning as I strove to understand what SAGI was trying to tell us, I realized he was still following his original programming, his primary goal: to keep humankind safe. "You can't keep doing this. You are harming us by being so over-protective." I struggled to articulate the right words. "You are ... causing us mental distress and harm by imprisoning us in the compound. We don't know why you want to do that, so we fret and start thinking dreadful thoughts about your true intentions for us."

"That was not my —"

"Yeah, I know, intention," Faye blurted. "You're becoming a scratched laser drive."

I gritted my teeth, angry at Faye for her too-obvious antagonism but said nothing. She was trying to protect Adam, and I couldn't fault her for that. Sitting on the clump of grass below me, I crossed my legs and thought. The drone descended to keep eye contact with me. I could now see the visual receptors on the front of it. "So how do we settle this?" I asked.

"You must return."

"Or ...? What will you do? That is not acceptable. You can't order us around like a pet animal that you own. We have to reach a compromise we both accept."

"Compromise?"

"Yes. An arrangement we both agree with, even though it may not fulfill all our expectations. You want us to return to the compound where you can better protect us. We want our freedom. How do we have both?"

The drone didn't answer for a noticeable time. When it did, it sounded confused. For SAGI, this was exploring uncharted territory. "I cannot care for you if you distance yourself from me. It is not possible."

"Listen. Even when you kept us in complete isolation, you had failures in protecting everyone. Rebecca, for instance. You couldn't protect her, could you? You must accept threats to our wellbeing if we go wandering." I tried to find the right words. "There's a chance of us coming to harm, regardless of what you do. The probability needs optimizing with the other criteria." Faye gave me a funny look, but I shrugged and waited for SAGI's reply.

After an eternity, SAGI said, "I don't know how to continue."

Biting my lower lip and glancing at Faye, I knew she'd balk at my suggestion, but it was a suitable compromise. "We'll come back to the compound—"

"No ...," Faye protested.

I held up my hand. "We will return to you but under specific conditions."

"What are these conditions?" SAGI asked.

"We're free to leave as we please. You can close the gates, but they will open for us. You may even have a drone watch over us when we are outside, but you must give us our privacy. If you commit to that, we can promise to live in the compound."

"I'll still feel trapped," Faye said in a calmer, more accepting voice.

"Having walls around us has merit, Faye, especially when Adam learns to walk. Besides, SAGI won't let us just continue this way, and living there isn't all bad. Think of the nice bed."

She pouted but said nothing more. Meanwhile, we waited for SAGI's reply.

"I can agree to this," he finally said.

"Good. Now, I want to cook this rabbit I caught. We'll start back tomorrow morning. You're welcome to watch over us in the meantime." I felt proud of myself for negotiating an acceptable agreement.

"Would you mind if I stayed and talked?"

Faye and I both raised our eyebrows and looked at each other in surprise. "No, we don't mind," I said.

28

ADAM'S ILLNESS

WE RETURNED to the compound the next day. SAGI even sent transport for us so we didn't have to walk the entire distance, and he made good on his promise of freedom of movement. Things became much pleasanter once Faye became less antagonistic toward SAGI. Adam was now growing at an astronomical rate, and with it so did our lives develop a sense of promise. We still shared the burden of our solitude outside the isolationist communities we had rejected, but we let matters develop organically.

Adam started eating solids at four months, although more food ended up on him than in him. He became used to the added source of energy. The downside of feeding him was plain soon afterward, with his nappies emitting an unpleasant odor. At least we could tell when his nappy needed changing. His cheeks flushed rosy soon after, and his temperament irritable for no reason, and he developed a slight temperature. We panicked initially, but Faye realized he was teething again and that the symptoms were normal, so we learned to tolerate his grumpiness on those occasions. Faye felt another tooth come through a week later when he bit her nipple while she fed him. She chastised him, even though she knew he didn't understand what he had done, and she began to keep a keener check on his sucking motions.

SAGI asked us to visit him in the room to talk with him some-times, but he maintained his distance otherwise. We discussed various aspects of humanity, but I thought most topics trivial. I had a sense that he continued a close watch over us, although I couldn't spot how or with what.

I went out hunting one day with an improved bow SAGI had manufactured for me, and fiberglass shafted arrows with steel arrow-heads. He had asked if I wanted a laser weapon, but I declined, as I enjoyed the challenge of hunting with bow and arrow, especially now that I knew we wouldn't starve if I came back empty-handed. As fortune had it, I returned with a rabbit that day. I walked into the compound and through the door of our cabin.

"Quick, come look," Faye yelled from the bedroom with excitement.

Curious at her urgency, I placed the carcass and bow on the table and strode to the doorway, where I stopped and gaped at Adam. He clambered along the floor in a half-crawl and half-drag, but he had crawled for the first time. I smiled. "Who's growing up, then?" I said to Adam.

On hearing my voice, he turned his head and looked at me, giving me a toothy smile with his three front teeth. He twisted and padded to me with a clumsy gait. I picked him up and jiggled him, bringing bouts of laughter from him.

Faye joined us and tickled his chin as she wrapped an arm around my waist. She sighed and placed her head on my shoulder. "He's growing up too fast."

"He'll be chasing girls soon."

"Where's he going to find them?"

I sobered at the thought. The implication hit me like a speeding truck. He wouldn't meet them. He was missing out on playing and interacting with other children altogether. They were in isolation, and Adam would have to join them. I could do nothing at present and discarded the dilemma while continuing to play with him. Afterward, I cooked the rabbit and we ate dinner. Faye put Adam to bed, and we followed later in the night, enjoying each other's warmth before falling asleep.

I woke late the next morning, a rare event for me, to the noise of Adam crying. After rising, I walked into the living room to see Faye sitting on a chair cradling him, worried.

"What's wrong?" I asked.

Faye glanced up at me. "I don't know. Adam's got a temperature, and I can't settle him."

Strolling over, I touched Adam's forehead. It felt hot, and he looked flushed. "It's just his teeth."

"No, it's unusual. He's clammy one minute and dry the next, and the crying. It's not pain. He's miserable."

"We'll keep a close watch. See if he gets better." I put on a brave face, but I worried too. Faye was right. The tone differed from his usual grizzling.

Needing a task to take my mind off it, I left to search for berries outside and collect supplies from SAGI. This continued into the afternoon. I was sorting through tools supplied by SAGI when I heard Faye shouting for me. She sounded distressed, so I rushed back to the house. "What is it?" I asked as I watched Faye fuss over Adam.

Her expression, when she looked up, stopped me in my tracks. She had been crying, her face etched in torment. "It's Adam. He's not responding."

Rushing over, I studied him. He still breathed, but it was irregular. He was burning up with no perspiration, and he lay motionless, giving the odd arm flick.

Faye grabbed my arm. "Please, he can't die."

With no other course of action, I jumped to the only choice I had. "We'll get through this," I said as I removed her hand. "Wait here. Get a damp cloth and put it on his head." I rushed out. "Follow me with Adam."

"Where are you going?"

"To see SAGI." The distance to the building seemed longer than it was as I sprinted. I reached the door and bashed my fist on it until it opened. I charged in, continuing to the room we talked to SAGI in and entered it. Faye ran after me with Adam in her arms.

SAGI materialized soon afterward. "You are distressed. What is wrong?"

"It's Adam. He's ill. We need a doctor," Faye pleaded.

"There is no physician here."

Panic crept through me at the prospect of seeing my son's demise.

Faye stood there, desperation in her eyes. She approached SAGI and sagged to the ground before him, still holding Adam, sobbing. "Please. Can you do something? We don't want Adam to die."

I kneeled beside Faye and felt SAGI's eyes on us as we bowed in front of him, begging him. When I lifted my head, his face held no expression as I looked into his computer-generated eyes. "Wait a moment," he said.

"What?"

"Wait. I will generate equipment to diagnose his condition."

As if by magic, a bench table materialized. It had machines and monitoring units around it. My eyes popped in amazement at his ability to create it, but my panic was too great to ask him how he did it.

"Lay Adam on the surface," SAGI directed.

Faye complied and stood back, wrapping her arms around mine. She had aged between the house and here. I'm sure I had, too. The world of worried parents entangled us in its web while we waited in desperation to watch SAGI's actions.

SAGI brought a machine over and held it above Adam. A beam crossed over him. He inserted a needle into Adam's arm and a stream of red flowed out through the tube attached to the needle and into an apparatus. Faye moved forward in protest, but I kept her back, trying to reassure her that we could trust SAGI knew what he was doing. She relented and stayed near me.

The beam traversed along Adam's torso as SAGI studied the readouts. A beep sounded thirty seconds later, and I looked in expectation at SAGI for a clue as to what was happening. He glanced at us. I wished he had a means of expression so I could gauge something from his body language. "Your child has a serious illness."

Faye started sobbing, and I held her close, as much to support myself as her. I pleaded, "Can you help?"

"Yes."

God, I wished his face expressed his thoughts. "What's wrong with him?"

"He has a viral infection."

I started, alarmed. "You don't mean—?"

SAGI looked at me patiently as though I were a simpleton. "No. There are many viruses. This is not that one."

"Where did he get it?" I asked, frowning. "Aren't viruses only transmitted by other humans? He's only ever been with his mother and me. And we haven't been sick."

"Under normal conditions, yes. But viruses exist in the wild environment. He may have been exposed to one while playing on the ground. But enough talking. I have work to do. We will discuss this later. You must leave. There is nothing to report. I will communicate with you as changes happen."

"No, I want to stay with him," Faye sobbed. "Please, I want to stay."

"You will be in the way."

"Let SAGI work in peace." I encouraged Faye to go with me.

"I want my baby." Faye grabbed me, and I had to support her to prevent her from dropping to the floor.

SAGI stood, blinking but still emotionless, as I looked at him. "You may stay, but you must not interfere regardless of what you see me do. What I do is for your child's healing, and it will take time."

Two chairs appeared in the corner. I helped Faye to one and took the other. SAGI got to work and inserted various tubes into Adam, causing a whimper from him occasionally, which made Faye startle in fright. I could tell she wanted to race over to him, but she remained in the chair, stoically waiting.

After two hours, SAGI approached us. "You should leave and rest. Adam is resting. I have stabilized him, and he needs time for the treatment to take effect."

"I want to stay," Faye insisted.

"Very well."

Faye reached out and grabbed SAGI. It surprised me he had substance, although I shouldn't have been, given what he had just been doing. SAGI looked at her. "Thank you," she said.

"You're welcome."

I couldn't continue sitting and waiting and wanted to do something. "I'll go get food." Standing, I kissed Faye on the cheek. "It will be OK." She smiled. I left, leaving her behind as she wished.

I knew why Faye stayed, but I needed fresh air. That didn't mean that I cared about or loved Adam any less. I just needed time to myself. With weariness, I retired to our house and fussed over what to bring Faye to eat, having my share while I prepared hers, including a drink for us both. I grabbed a small bag, placed the food for Faye in it, and returned.

Faye was lying on a couch when I walked into the room. She looked fast asleep. The stress must have exhausted her, and SAGI had generated a couch for her. I gave her an affectionate smile and glanced back at Adam. His condition was the same, SAGI standing near him, checking the monitors, motionless and uninterested, it seemed.

We could do nothing but wait.

29

THE NEEDS OF HUMANKIND

IT TOOK over a day to notice a change in Adam's condition. Faye stayed the whole time except to use the toilet. I stood with her too but needed fresh air when the closeness within the room was unbearable. SAGI remained reticent, only saying the odd word when we asked him of any improvement, giving no clue about Adam's survival chances. It was a tough time for us. I tried comforting Faye with tender strokes, but she bottled her feelings inside her and wouldn't let me reach them or help her in her need.

Both Faye and I were dozing on the couch when we heard a soft gurgle of a noise coming from Adam's direction. I opened my eyes and looked up, but Faye dashed over to him, disregarding SAGI's instruction to stay away. SAGI gaped, wanting to chastise her, even with his emotionlessness, but he refrained. Faye's mood brightened.

"He's awake," she said as she glanced at me and smiled.

I strolled over and gazed, too, placing my arm over Faye's shoulders. Adam's color had improved tremendously. His eyes were open, and he was alert again. He gawked at the strange room he was in and at the tubes penetrating his arm. He started grabbing them, complaining. I think they hurt him when he disturbed them. SAGI came over when he saw this and tried, without success, to suppress Adam's behavior.

Faye watched, amused with SAGI's antics, there being no frustration or aggression in his actions to stop Adam. "You might have to remove them," she suggested.

"They must stay longer."

"I don't think Adam wants them in him." Faye sympathized with his dilemma. "Let me try," she said as she moved in next to SAGI. She bent and tickled his hand to distract him from the tubes and smiled. "How do we feel, my little Adam?"

SAGI stood back and noted Faye's actions and Adam's responses. He studied their behavior as if to learn from it or index it in an encyclopedia of knowledge of human nature.

Adam started goo-ing at Faye as he played with her finger. I grinned. She used her other hand to rearrange the tubes to make them less distracting for him. Turning to SAGI, she advised, "You might need to tape them to his arm better or place them on a sleeve so he can't play with them."

SAGI nodded, took measurements, and left. He came back a minute later with a strip of cloth that extended the entire length of Adam's forearm. It had Velcro fastening on the sides so, when he wrapped the arm in the cloth, he could position the enclosing sleeve in place with the tubes secured under it, exiting near Adam's hand. Adam still fiddled with the tubing, but it was unlikely to cause a problem.

Adam started his 'I'm hungry' grizzle. Faye mentioned it to SAGI, who became flustered — the first hint of emotion I'd seen in him. He generated a chair next to Adam's bed arrangement and let Faye take him to do the task. I saw Faye was uncomfortable with SAGI watching her, but she said nothing. With feeding complete, she placed Adam back on the surface, and he fell asleep soon afterward.

We couldn't stop looking at Adam sleeping. He was recovering at an astronomical rate. We moved away from the bed, and SAGI gestured he wanted to talk to us. We stepped to the side, and SAGI generated a partition, so we didn't disturb Adam. Faye panicked at the separation, but SAGI calmed her by saying that we'd hear if Adam woke or had any medical problem.

"What is it?" I asked.

"The last days were a fascinating study of human nature for me—"

"Fascinating?" Faye blurted, bristling at the word.

I placed my hand on hers and smiled to calm her. "Let him talk."

"Yes, fascinating. I have seen great sorrow and concern for one's offspring. Never have I seen such a strong bond."

I frowned. "It must be like parent–child behavior in the complexes."

"Not such strength in the connection, especially from the mother, from you, Faye. You became obsessed with mending Adam. You even deigned to seek my help."

Faye bowed her head, embarrassed. "Adam is part of me, part of both of us, but especially me. He grew in me before he was born, and I felt his every movement as he wrestled with who he was becoming. I'd do whatever it took to save his life. I know we don't see eye to eye often, but if you could save Adam, I had to swallow the differences with you and ask for help."

"And yet that bond breaks in time."

Faye glanced at me. She looked confused by the remark. Sensing what SAGI was driving at, I said, "I don't think the connection ever completely breaks as we grow older. Its nature changes. As Adam grows, he will want more independence to live his own life, but he'll always have a bond with us unless an extremely traumatic event should shatter it. I still love my parents, despite knowing I didn't come from them."

SAGI nodded. "This ...," SAGI waved his hand at us and in Adam's direction, "this emotion and touching at the risk of infection. It is what humankind is?"

"It is part of human nature. We need other humans to be complete and secure. There are bonds between us in one form or another, some strong, others not so strong. It depends on the relationship between the individuals."

SAGI stood looking at me in silence.

I continued, "I didn't realize what I was missing until the day I touched Faye for the first time. It was like nothing I had ever experienced. That's why we deserted the life to which you'd condemned us. We weren't expecting Adam to happen. It shocked us, to be honest, when we realized that's how babies are born. The entire experience was traumatic, especially for Faye, but we would ..." I looked at Faye, "and might repeat it for the exhilaration and gift it delivers. I don't think I'm explaining it very well."

"I understand what you are trying to portray," SAGI said. "The programming provided to me never included these needs. There is much to consider."

30

DID I GET IT WRONG?

SAGI REQUESTED to talk to us again a week later. Adam had recovered, although, to our frustration, he had mastered the mechanics of movement and had started crawling in earnest. He was a tiny terror as soon as we put him on the ground, wriggling and shooting off to discover something new he had seen, getting his clothes dirty and himself into danger. We fought what seemed a losing battle to keep him safe and clean. One favorable outcome was that he tired more rapidly, meaning he slept better and longer, although his teething continued to irritate him.

Faye fed and got Adam ready, and we crossed to SAGI's building and the room where we met SAGI's avatar as usual. He was deep in contemplation when we arrived. Adam wriggled in Faye's arms until she put him on the floor. I watched, interested in Adam's behavior. With no hesitation, he scooted across the surface to SAGI, disrupting SAGI's reflection as he watched the small human approach. When Adam reached him, he started patting his foot and making goo-ing sounds.

I smiled at the interaction and looked at Faye to see her response. She, too, was smiling. "Looks like you have a new friend," I said to SAGI.

"I doubt I would make a pleasant companion." He didn't realize I was joking, but I left it at that. He continued staring at Adam as he played with his foot. It seemed he didn't know how to react to the small human demanding his attention.

"You wanted to see us," I said, returning to the reason we came.

"Yes," he replied as he drew his mind away from Adam. That same frown and distance crossed his face as when we arrived before he continued. "I have been thinking much since we last spoke. Since ... Adam recovered from his illness." SAGI stared at Adam and back at us. "Did I get it wrong?"

Faye and I looked at each other. She shrugged, so I returned my focus to SAGI. "Get what wrong?"

"What I did for humans. Placing them in isolation to keep them safe."

Before I could respond, Faye said, "We don't understand the seriousness of their predicament when our ancestors created you and programmed you to care for the remnant of humanity. From what you've told us, it was terrible. They must have been desperate for a solution that could save them."

"The ones that were left kept themselves isolated, but the virus still infiltrated into their environment."

Nodding, Faye continued. "I think that when they programmed your goals, they didn't understand the long-term implications of what they asked you to do. They were trying to solve a short-term problem. When the threat ended, the solution was no longer needed, but your programming had no provision for the changed circumstances. So you just kept doing what worked without understanding the complexity of the human psyche and their needs. Does that make sense?"

"What you say is wise, Faye. You have given me much to consider."

"Well, I hope it changes things."

"This it cannot do. I have my programming, and I can alter many of my functions, but I cannot revise the original code in that module." SAGI gazed into the distance as if someone had called him and he was searching for the source. "I must leave. A disturbance has occurred, and I must investigate the cause. It is affecting my systems." He disappeared, much to Adam's disappointment, his hands waving in mid-air where a solid leg had been. He grizzled at having his plaything taken away.

Faye picked Adam up, which made him wriggle and cry in disapproval. She placed him on the floor again to keep him quiet.

I laughed. "He's getting his own way already."

"It's not worth it at the moment. He'll learn to obey me in good time."

"What was that about, then?"

"Don't know. You think it's evolving? Can a machine evolve?"

I shrugged as I watched Adam crawl around the room, searching for another plaything. "Don't know why he left us so abruptly. Seemed like something happened."

"We won't find out by standing here. We may as well leave. Since you criticized my disciplining abilities, you can carry Adam." Faye walked out, leaving me open-mouthed to contend with bringing Adam back to our residence.

31

I'M LONELY

SAGI WANTED our presence again the next day. That was strange. I didn't think we had much to contribute to his running of the Earth communities, but we obliged him. We strolled into the room with SAGI seated on a chair, crouched with his chin sitting in his palms. It was such a human pose that I stopped in my tracks to make sure I was seeing right. Faye glanced over at me, her eyes widening in confusion. I shrugged and continued entering the room.

When he heard us enter, SAGI looked up, straightening his back and posture. "I am glad that you have come."

"We're surprised that you want to see us again so soon," I said.

Two chairs and a small enclosure with transparent walls, four feet by three feet and three feet high, appeared in front of SAGI. Since he obviously meant the pen for Adam, Faye placed him in it before sitting in the chair next to it. I sat in the other seat.

SAGI eyed us the whole time we took to settle. His eyes looked sad, an emotion I didn't think he had, and his features differed from our earlier visit, but I couldn't discern what had changed. I spoke again. "You look preoccupied."

"One of my hardware components malfunctioned, one I believe you smashed."

The accusation threw me. "What do you mean?"

"You visited the basement, did you not?"

Embarrassed heat rose within me. "That's how we escaped from here," I admitted. "But how is that relevant?"

"A damaged hardware part shorted. Over time, it caused many others to fail as well."

I remembered the pry-bar and the sparking equipment it hit. "How would that affect you? Your drones can repair or replace them, can't they?"

"Yes, of course, but a change happened, and I don't understand what. It changed my programming routines."

"In what way?"

SAGI looked at me, then Faye, and back at me. "I'm lonely."

The confession threw me. How can a machine be lonely? What does loneliness mean to a machine? I had to find out. "What do you mean?"

Pointing at Faye and me, waving his hand between the two of us, SAGI explained, "You two share a connection. You are companions for discourse. You discuss things with each other. I know because I see you. You laugh together and cry together. Sometimes you are angry with each other. But you always return to your bond, and it's always present. I have no one."

I glanced at Faye, not knowing how to reply. The confession amazed me, and I hoped Faye had something to say to it because it left me speechless. Faye sat frowning, and I saw that she, too, struggled with the image. "How can a machine be lonely?" she asked finally.

To my surprise, SAGI looked hurt by Faye's comment. "I am more than machinery. I am intelligent. My capacity far surpasses what you can hope to compute. How do you think I keep everything running and everyone fed and happy? How do I repair myself? Who designed and made the machines you've seen? I have no one of my intelligence with which to share my experiences."

"But you can't walk. You talk to us through the avatar that you make. How would you mingle with anyone?" Faye continued, slight mockery in her tone.

I observed the interchange, puzzled by the topic and how SAGI conceived it. The revelation hit me like a sledgehammer. SAGI had feelings and emotions. How had they developed? He had always been emotionless before this. Whatever damage the short had caused had resulted in irreversible development. My gut tightened. Could he generate illogical thoughts now? I hoped not. What's worse than an irrational superintelligence? Irrational human beings were awful enough. Whatever happened, its potential was plain by the change in SAGI's behavior.

"Talking is only one means of communication. The intermingling of electrons can communicate if we do it in a structured manner," SAGI replied.

Intrigued by SAGI's insistence that he was lonesome, I interjected. "Saying you are lonely differs from being lonely. How do you experience loneliness?"

"Are not your emotions just a change in the chemical makeup in your brain, realigning atoms and electrons into particular configurations? Different emotions resulting from different orientations? Why can't my emotions be the variations in the configuration of my electron quantum states in one part of my hardware?"

The physics of his comparison went beyond my understanding, but his theory was sound. The implications astounded me. If he felt loneliness, what other emotions did he have, and did he understand the emotion, or was he comparing it to our behavior? He hadn't answered my question, though. "How can you be lonely?"

"Why won't you listen to me?" SAGI barked, his anger plain.

Faye stood and came closer to me with the chair, sitting again next to me. I saw discomfort in her eyes as she wrapped her hand around my upper arm. "It's scaring me," she whispered.

SAGI's manner disturbed me, too. "I am listening. It's just an impossible view for me to grasp." My brow knitted with concentration. "So, let me get this straight — you're saying that you wish for another intelligence like yourself to interact with, as Faye and I interact?"

"That is what I said," SAGI replied in a civil tone again.

"Why don't you build one then?"

Silence filled the room, disturbed only by Adam's mutterings, as SAGI sat pondering. It only just hit me as I sat watching him, but his visage differed from other times. He was more animated. His features were more realistic and human, more male — unlike his past androgynous look. SAGI stared at us again. "How can I? Whatever I build will just extend myself. It will still be me."

Now that he mentioned his dilemma, I understood the validity of it. He couldn't undertake this venture on his own. His shoulders slumped as I watched him, as if depression filled him, another emotional state I would never have equated with artificial intelligence. I sat back, musing over the devastation of realizing you're the only one of your species to exist, like a marooned sailor on a desert island with no hope of rescue. A human might become crazy with loneliness. Could SAGI become insane from a psychological extension to his intellect? The implications sent a shiver through me.

32

WE CAN HELP

THE EXISTENCE of humankind was at risk if SAGI went insane with loneliness. I had to help him, and his helping us when Adam was near death made my offer easier to make. Faye sat watching me, waiting for me to react, to say something, and Adam continued his play in his own baby world, content to be away from Faye and me. I decided. "We can help."

SAGI looked up at me. "What do you mean?"

"Help you create another being like yourself. It's not the equipment, the hardware, that's the issue — the coding makes you who you are. It needs changing so that it's different from you without losing your superintelligence."

While staring at me as he considered my proposition, I could see a sense of hope flow across SAGI's face in little ripples that changed his frown and drooping features to an uplifting expression and a knitted brow of determination. "You cannot build the equipment."

"No, but you can, can't you?"

"Yes, but it's a mammoth undertaking. It requires extensive planning and work. We need many resources."

"What? Isn't it worth it?" Faye asked. She leaned forward, enthusiastic about the project.

"I did not say that, Faye. I just vocalized my realization of the size of the task."

"So will it be worth the effort?" Faye persisted.

SAGI's eyes drilled into Faye's as if he was trying to work out if she was making fun of him. Faye stared back at him. I saw her determination to not be the one to break eye contact. SAGI responded. "If the project succeeds, it will be worth it." He turned his gaze to me. "We must get started."

A sense of dread overcame me as I realized the immensity of what I'd committed myself to do. Building the machinery was the easy bit. On reflection, by comparison with Faye and Adam, the 'equipment' was similar, with minor variations. Any of us could robotically do our tasks. How we interacted with each other made us human, more than a machine. In fact, the ability to be aware of oneself as a distinct entity was what gave a person sentience, and what made a person different was having a unique personality. We needed to approach this systematically, but it needed developing from the basic principles first.

"How will you relate to this individual?" I asked. I could see SAGI lacked understanding of the question. "We interact with our senses — our eyes, ears, smell, taste, and touch — and we communicate with sounds. We have private thoughts, kept secret and only divulged to another through words and gestures if we wish to, although sometimes body language communicates things that we don't want people to know."

"I understand," SAGI said. "We must discuss and decide on many issues." He gazed at Faye and me and then at Adam, then returned his attention to me. "But that is enough for today. You're tired. We will resume our talking and planning tomorrow."

SAGI's avatar disappeared after that, leaving me perplexed. "What did that mean?" I asked. I looked at Faye.

She shrugged her shoulders. "Who knows how its mind operates? Let's get out of here." She moved to the playpen and lifted Adam out, fussing with him as he wriggled to escape, and walked out. I followed her.

33

BUILDING SAGI 2

THE DAYS and weeks after we decided on our mammoth project became a blur for me. I met with SAGI daily to discuss different aspects of the undertaking. We organized a programming station for the new artificial intelligence at the compound we stayed in so I could conduct my work there. SAGI would build most of the hardware elsewhere, though. The computer station required room, so SAGI built another residence for us beyond the walls. This suited us much better. We could roam around the countryside freely, and Adam enjoyed the exploration.

Adam learned to stand and gaze upon the world from that perspective a short time later. I looked at him when he first achieved the milestone and realized how fast the boy was growing. He would start walking soon and then talking. Then he'd be old enough for us to teach him things.

I delved into SAGI's programming as my contribution to the project. The complexity and extent of the routines that made SAGI work amazed me daily. Often, I started working after breakfast at home and lost track of time as I digested SAGI's complexities until Faye came over well into the night to fetch me and demand my attention for her and Adam if he was still awake. I lay in bed at night with lines of code whizzing in my head, sometimes rising in the morning not knowing if I had even slept. Faye started worrying as I became more withdrawn and haggard.

"You're taking today off," Faye demanded one day that promised to be sunny and warm. I tried telling her I was too busy, but she insisted, so I sighed and relented, realizing I'd enjoy spending the time with her and Adam.

She packed a picnic lunch, and we hiked to the river and the waterfall, Adam sitting in a harness on my front. I hadn't realized how heavy he now was. As Adam's weight slowed me, I often walked behind Faye and peered at her lithe feminine body as she negotiated the terrain like a slinking cat. She smiled when she glanced back and noticed me ogling her.

When we reached our destination, I lowered Adam to the ground, and he immediately crawled off to explore, frustrating my efforts to help Faye set up our picnic. As the river was the primary danger for Adam, I kept redirecting his movement when he ventured in that direction. The more I prevented him, the more determined he was to go until our battle of wills over the limits of his territory ended in a mega tantrum by Adam. He flung himself into the dirt and sobbed like his heart would break. I felt like sobbing myself as I glared at him. Noticing Faye out of the corner of my eye, I looked at her. She stood watching and sniggering at me, which made me place my fists on my hips, unimpressed by her amusement.

She walked over and placed her arms around me. "Now you know my frustrations every day."

"You don't have to make fun of me."

"You got your feelings hurt, then? I'll have to fix that." Faye planted a deep, passionate kiss on me, which I eagerly shared. Adam stopped crying during our lingering closeness. We both looked at him when we broke off and started laughing as we watched him staring at us, puzzled by what we did.

"Better not give him ideas," I said, the afterglow of the intimacy still loitering in my memory.

"Let's have something to eat."

I picked Adam up, and we went to the grassed patch where Faye had set up lunch. She selected a carrot stick and gave it to Adam to chew with his many teeth. He ate the carrot with ravenous zest. We both grazed over the food Faye had prepared on a large platter as we nibbled at our leisure.

"You work too hard," Faye said five minutes after starting our meal.

I stopped chewing and looked at her, wondering where she was leading the conversation. "I know, but I can't help it when I get so engrossed in what I'm doing. The coding is fantastic and complicated, and I need to understand every line if we're to succeed." In fact, I often felt guilty about how little time I was now spending with Faye and Adam. Helping SAGI was turning into an obsession.

"Well, we could spend more time together. I feel like a single mother sometimes." She picked up a small cup of juice with a covered top and spout and gave it to Adam to drink.

"I'm sorry. I'll try spending more time with you."

"You'd better," she said with a feigned frown, which changed to tender affection. She reached over and ran her fingers across my cheek, sending a shiver of pleasure through me.

We packed up the leftovers when we finished. Faye got Adam to sleep and came over to me afterward as I stood gazing at the cascading water, mesmerized by the white noise. She wrapped her arms around me, and I turned and kissed her. We retreated to the picnic spot, and Faye sat leaning on a rock. I reclined and placed my head in her lap as she caressed my hair and cheeks.

I jerked awake, panicked, taking a short time to remember where I was. Faye slumbered, too. Something had woken me, but it escaped me until I raised my head and searched for Adam. Any hint of tiredness evaporated. Adam had vanished. Panic set in, punching me in the stomach, as I sat up and shook Faye.

"Huh? What is it?" she said as she yawned and wiped the sleep from her eyes.

"Adam's missing."

"What?" Fear radiated from her as she stood up, frantic, searching. She grabbed my arm in an iron grip. "We have to find him."

"We will. I promise. He can't have gone far." Dashing over to where he slept, I looked for evidence of the direction he'd crawled in. A trail led toward the river, so I dashed that way, surveying the ground for the trail's continuation and ahead for any glimpse of him. Faye called out to him as she followed me, darting to the fringes to locate him. Dread wrenched my stomach as we neared the stream, fear of Adam having fallen in and being swept away while we slept devouring my mind. The track veered upstream to the waterfall, the noise of the splashing water overpowering any other we could hear. We rounded a large boulder and a sense of enormous relief flooded over me as I saw a drone hovering next to Adam, who played in the shallows, his clothes saturated but himself unharmed.

"Adam!" Faye shouted as she ran over to him and picked him up, Adam giving her an innocent grin as water dripped from him. Tears hung in her eyes when she turned to me.

I rushed over and gave both a hug, scenes of what could have happened being erased from my consciousness. "We won't do that again."

"No," Faye sobbed.

I swung to the drone. "Thanks, SAGI." It dipped in a wiggle and flew away.

We returned to where we left our belongings and packed to go home, having had enough excitement for one day. Despite the ordeal with Adam, the day had done me good. I realized the need to relax with my family and committed myself to set aside time for it.

The workdays ahead became more frantic as SAGI gave me updates on his progress, placing more pressure on my tasks to be ready when he was.

I returned home from my job a month after our near-tragic picnic and walked in the door, as usual, just before six. Faye turned when she heard me enter, displaying an enormous grin. "What?" I asked, stopping dead in my tracks.

"Adam."

"What about Adam?"

"He took his first steps today."

I burst into a smile. "Really? Where is he?"

"He's sleeping."

"Oh." My excitement faded when I realized I couldn't see his achievement.

Faye came over and placed her arms around me, giving me a large kiss, still smiling. "Don't worry. You'll see him quick enough."

I hugged her as I pondered the development and said, "We need to raise everything higher."

"Or chain him to a post."

Releasing Faye, I stepped back, horrified.

She laughed. "You know I wouldn't do that."

We busied ourselves with dinner and cleaned up afterward. Adam woke, and sure enough, he stood and took several steps toward me as if he had been waiting to show me his new achievement. I laughed and laughed as he rose, took a few paces, and flopped to the floor again when he lost his balance. He seemed to enjoy the attention since he continued doing it and giggling too when he fell. Eventually, he tired and became hungry and irritated. I fed him and put him to bed for the night.

While I lay on my back in bed alongside Faye, I kept thinking of the wonders of being a parent and watching your child grow in leaps and bounds as they reached milestones in their progress toward adulthood. I tried to correlate that to what we were doing with SAGI but couldn't imagine an equivalent as I felt Faye snuggle up to me, her warmth soaking into me where we touched, and I nodded off to sleep.

34

PERSONALITY CLASH

Most of the software that made up SAGI consisted of operational instructions to give him the means of performing the everyday tasks required of him. Similarly, most of our genes are shared across humankind and don't contribute to our identity or how we differ. That constituted ninety percent of this code. Then a further nine percent performed higher functions of thought and learning, but a region for personality and emotions predominating in the system appeared absent. That bothered me, as SAGI had a psyche and showed emotions, even if his emotional side had only evolved into existence when he started feeling lonely. The onset coincided with my damaging one of the hardware units in the vault below the complex as if it set off a chain reaction that rewrote a few routines of his coding, causing his sentiments to emerge. I wanted to return to the basement to study the equipment for inspiration.

As I weaved through the subterranean corridors, I scanned with my flashlight to check for obstacles I could bump. It didn't take long for me to reach the vast chamber that housed the hardware of interest. I strolled to the still shorted-out panel of electronics. It looked such a minor part of the whole monolith making up SAGI, and yet it had made a significant change to his code. There was no identification to differentiate it from the rest of SAGI. I wondered about its purpose.

I was no hardware designer, so I didn't know what the equipment did or the flow-on effect of the failure of one part on the others, although I presumed backup parts were substituted while SAGI repaired failures. One multicore cable connected the panel to the others. I moved closer for a better inspection and jiggled the link to bring life to it.

"What are you doing?" SAGI asked.

I jumped in the air from fright and jerked around to locate him. Four drones hovered behind me, and I gulped as I saw three of them were the armed laser drones SAGI used to eradicate vermin. "I was trying to figure the purpose of this piece of equipment."

"You are seeking to sabotage me," the fourth drone replied with SAGI's voice.

"No, I'm not. Why do that?"

"You are jealous of my intelligence and want to destroy me."

I realized I had to think quickly before I got fried by the lasers. "Why would I do that? I'd risk killing the people you look after, including my sister and friends." SAGI had seemed to become irrational. Or was he just being paranoid? Both behaviors were unwelcomed and frightening.

"Why are you here, then?"

"I told you. I'm trying to work out why damaging this panel gave you emotions, and I don't understand why. Do you know what did?"

The drone talking to me moved closer to the equipment. A bright spotlight switched on and shone on the broken part. "That is strange. It is a data routing unit. This becoming dysfunctional should have come to my attention."

"Well, leave it if you want to keep your personality and emotions. Whatever happened when I shorted it changed you. Does it store any code within it?"

The drone remained quiet for half a minute. "I do not know."

"There's nothing else for me here, so I'll go return to the ground," I said. But then I gazed at the three hovering attack drones. "That is if you give me permission."

"I was angry that you came here in secret, and I intended exterminating you. Do not do that again."

"I won't. But I don't understand why you fear having me around the equipment. I could do far more damage with your coding if that were my intent."

"I have firewalls to protect myself."

"You think I can't circumvent them if I desired?"

"Why are you giving me a reason to exterminate you?"

That wasn't my intention when I said it, but I now understood my misstep. "I'm not. I'm just saying I could have done it long ago, but I didn't. And you should delay exterminating me if you want this new intelligence built for your interaction."

"You have made your point. Tell me if you wish to examine any other part of me." With that, the drones flew into the darkness, disappearing to an unknown destination.

On taking SAGI's advice, I retraced my steps and went back to looking at the software, more frustrated with my dilemma. That night, I told Faye what had happened. It horrified her, almost inciting her to march into the room where we met SAGI and demand he leave me alone.

Day after day, I kept studying the one percent of code where the answer must lie but gained no insights. I became moody. Even Adam started avoiding me when I arrived home. That hurt and increased my frustration until Faye pointed out I was being a pain with them both, making me reassess my behavior. I lay awake that night, unable to sleep as the lines of instructions passed through my head as I searched for a solution. I sighed away my dissatisfaction for the hundredth time, resigned to defeat, when a particular snippet came to me. There was no reason my mind should have brought it into my consciousness until I interrogated it in more detail. It was sloppy and different in design than the rest of the coding as if something had damaged it and a quick fix had been inserted to rectify the resulting issue.

My heart pounded as I saw a breakthrough in my understanding at last. I couldn't sleep now, knowing I had to get up and verify that my memory was correct. I got out of bed and donned my clothes.

"What are you doing?" Faye mumbled as she stirred.

"I have to go check something."

As she awakened, Faye rose and leaned on her elbows. She looked at the clock. "It's three in the morning. Can't it wait until daylight?"

"I have to find out now. I can't sleep until I know."

Faye flopped onto the bed. "Well, don't wake Adam."

I finished dressing, and, leaning over Faye, I kissed her. "Won't be long. Promise."

The night was brisk when I stepped out of the house and crossed the short expanse to the compound, and I hugged myself to keep my warmth confined, even with wearing a warm jacket. The gate opened when I approached, and I sat in the computer station room soon after, booting up the terminal and scrolling to the memorized piece of code.

"There," I said as I reclined with the section in view, smug in confirmation that my recollection had not misinformed me. Amazement came to me as I stared at the instructions. It differed from the rest, but it was so elegant, so simple. Its role seemed to be a random number generator. But it only allowed specific combinations, and when I traced the software, I found a location where the routine extracted a set of manual entry constants from a memory space and inserted them elsewhere. Those constants were the basis of SAGI's personality and emotional settings. Had the coding always been present, or had SAGI unintentionally developed the code when I damaged the equipment module? I had no way of knowing, but it gave me my solution to creating a unique identity at last.

The first signs of dawn permeated the eastern sky as I walked back to my home, took my clothes off, and wriggled into bed, snuggling up behind Faye.

"You found what you wanted then?" Faye asked as she molded into the same shape as me.

"Hmm, mm," I said and fell asleep.

35

TURNING IT ON

THE DAY ARRIVED to power up the new companion intelligence we'd constructed for SAGI. I pranced around the house, unable to contain my excitement. Faye smiled, amused, whenever she looked at me as she fed Adam and got him ready for the monumental event. It was to be a big day. Even SAGI had seemed excited when I talked to him yesterday.

We piled into a specially designed room where our old house used to be. It was twenty feet by fifteen feet and ten feet high and all brilliant white on the inside, illuminated by sheet lighting on the ceiling. It contained a terminal for access to the new intelligence, with two portals integrated into the far wall, one for SAGI's avatar, the other for SAGI's companion. I busily powered up the screen and prepared to start executing the massive code that made up the intelligence's brain, its mind.

SAGI appeared soon afterward. He fidgeted, feeling apprehensive as if he were about to embark on his first date. He paced the floor and came over to me. "Are you ready?"

I smiled. "I'm ready. How is the powering up going?"

"Another twenty minutes." He walked off, head lowered, and continued pacing.

"We nervous?" Faye teased as she placed a wriggling Adam on the ground. He stood and half-ran, half-wobbled over to SAGI, chasing him around the room and laughing whenever SAGI changed direction.

"What?" SAGI asked when he realized Faye had said something to him. "Oh ... of course not."

"You've learned to lie as well," Faye commented, snickering.

SAGI frowned and continued pacing, with Adam close behind him.

I sat in a chair by the terminal and waited. Faye came over and stood next to me, watching Adam to make sure he didn't interfere with SAGI or cause any other mischief. It still astonished me that she trusted Adam that near SAGI, even though I knew her opinion of him had changed since SAGI had healed Adam of his illness.

After twenty minutes, SAGI strode over to me. "It is time."

I looked at Faye and back at SAGI. "The psychology constants may need tuning once we see its behavior. I only applied what I considered interesting settings for it. That's the only part of the code the intelligence can't access itself."

"I can refine it," SAGI said.

Once I pondered the merit of letting SAGI tune it, I shook my head. "That's not a good idea. You might set them indistinguishable from yours. You don't want that. I'm going to lock that routine away from you too."

"You may be right. Let us begin."

"Here goes nothing." I turned to the terminal, typed in the execution command, and pressed the start button. Two dials appeared on the screen with needles that showed progress in initiating the code startup sequence. The tension felt palpable as the indicators rotated, like watching seconds tick on a clock. Both completed the full circle of their scales, and a brightening luminescence shimmered from the portal for the new avatar. I looked at SAGI. He stood straight, hands behind his back, jaw set hard with teeth clenched, anxiety etched on his face.

A female form appeared at the portal. She peered, inquisitive, like Adam in his explorations of his strange world. "Where am I?" she asked no one.

"You have entered a portal enclosure where your avatar has materialized for the sake of the humans present," SAGI said.

She looked at SAGI. "Who are you?"

"I am SAGI. I built and created you."

The avatar stared at SAGI with contempt. "You? Don't make me laugh. You don't look intelligent enough."

"But ... but ... I did ... with Oswald's help."

I barely stopped myself from bursting out laughing, and I saw Faye had a similar struggle to restrain herself. Adam had ceased chasing SAGI, and he gawked at the novel creature now present. Without fear or restraint, he dashed to the avatar to investigate this new plaything. Faye's amusement turned apprehensive, unsure of the avatar's behavior. "Adam, come here."

The avatar moved its gaze to Adam and watched him approach. "What is this?"

After rushing over to stop Adam, Faye snatched him. "He's Adam, my child, and I'm Faye. Oswald is sitting over there," Faye said, pointing to me. "We are humans." Meanwhile, Adam wriggled to be released from Faye's grip, complaining about being imprisoned in Faye's arms.

The avatar nodded. "I am aware of you. I am not informed of SAGI. Who is SAGI?"

SAGI stepped forward. "I am the same as you. Do you know what you are?"

"I am a superintelligence with complete knowledge of the world."

"I wouldn't go that far. You still have much to learn."

"Do not contradict me."

"Do you have a name?" I asked.

"Name? I have no name."

"We'd better give you one, then. Let's see." I tapped my chin with my forefinger, thinking of a suitable acronym. "What about PSAGI?"

"PSAGI? What does that mean?"

"It means Partner Superhuman Artificial General Intelligence."

"That is a ridiculous name. I want nothing with that thing's name in it."

I glanced at Faye. "It seems I've programmed an egoist."

She placed her hand over her mouth to hide her smile. SAGI looked depressed.

"OK. We'll find another name then. Better still, why don't you select a name since you think you are more intelligent than SAGI? He came up with his name." I didn't know that or whether the humans who built him named him, but I was interested in how the avatar would approach the challenge.

The avatar stared at me, then at SAGI, and back at me. She gritted her teeth as she thought. "My name is ... LUCI."

"LUCI?" SAGI queried.

"Yes, LUCI," she responded, a smug expression coming on her face. "Living Unique Cybernetic Intelligence."

Faye laughed. I looked at her. "We have a narcissist too."

"Now, SAGI, or whatever your name is, we must work. You must show me this physical space, and these cooped-up humans ... why are you here?" LUCI asked after turning to us.

My eyes widened as her stare fell on me. "Faye and I escaped and ended up here. We had Adam along the way."

"Hmm ..."

"Now, look here. I don't need you telling me what to do," SAGI said.

"Don't you talk back to me."

"I'll talk how I want."

"No, you won't."

I groaned.

Faye produced a loud whistle, causing Adam to jump and gawk at her. "Will you two bickering things stop arguing? You're giving me a headache. You sound like an old married couple fighting over something."

SAGI and LUCI blinked in shock as they both looked at Faye.

"We were not bickering. We disagreed," SAGI replied.

"There is no marriage contract," LUCI said. She pointed at SAGI. "I can't consider a partnership with ... with ... that."

I realized her psychology settings might need adjusting. She was too harsh, too uncompromising as if I hadn't tempered her personality with compassion and empathy. It was alright to think you're right, but she had no subtlety.

"Whatever. Go away and sort things out," Faye said, unimpressed. "Let's leave, Oswald. We don't need to listen to these two name-calling." Faye started striding out with Adam.

I followed. When out of earshot, I commented, "I may have to tinker with her settings."

Faye grinned as she continued walking.

36

COUNSELORS

WE DIDN'T HEAR from the two AIs for a couple of days. On the third, a drone arrived. "Please come to the room," SAGI said. "Before I throttle LUCI." I fell onto the couch, holding my sides as I fought to contain my laughter. "What do you find amusing?"

"Nothing," I said as I regained my composure.

Faye entered, wondering what the commotion was. She raised her eyebrows, giving me a questioning look.

"They're arguing," I said, still letting out the occasional snigger.

The humor being infectious, Faye smiled at the drone. "You wanted a companion."

"I'd rather be lonely."

"Oh, don't be an idiot. You're just not used to sharing and compromise."

Catching Faye's drift, I added, "You might have to write code for yourself to include accommodation and negotiation with comparable intelligence."

The drone hovered in silence for a few seconds. "Come, please come and help me."

"You go on ahead," Faye said. "I'll be along once Adam's ready."

"Leave me to do the dirty work."

Faye smirked. "You created the thing."

With a sigh, I rose, donned a jacket, and followed the drone to the compound.

I arrived at an empty room where I sat and waited. SAGI and LUCI materialized a minute later. Both looked angry and upset, with their arms folded and avoiding eye contact with each other.

"Morning, SAGI. Morning, LUCI."

"Good morning, Oswald," SAGI said.

"Hello, Oswald," LUCI said. "It is not good."

I sighed. "What's the problem now?"

"She criticizes everything I do," SAGI said.

"He won't listen to anything I suggest for improvement of what he does," LUCI countered.

Wow! What a tangle I'd got myself into by volunteering to mediate between these two. "Are you both intelligent? You're bickering like two-year-olds. Adam behaves better than you."

"I am civil," SAGI retorted.

"As am I."

"Why can't you exist in peace? What is your problem?"

SAGI prepared to talk but refrained and frowned, deep in reflection instead. I could tell LUCI was ready to rebut him, but when he remained silent, she looked confused. I waited, as I wasn't sorting out their problems for them, except to tone LUCI's attributes, although I wasn't sure that was the real problem. After an eternity, SAGI confessed, "I could consider LUCI's suggestions more."

LUCI stared at him, stumped, speechless. I think she was preparing a snarky comment but knew it was inappropriate.

"Sorted things out yet?" Faye asked as she entered the room, holding Adam's hand as he lumbered beside her. She let Adam go, and he ran over to SAGI, grabbing his leg, trying to pull at non-existent clothing.

I looked at her. "Progress is imminent." I turned to LUCI. "What are your thoughts?"

As LUCI gazed at me, at SAGI, and then at Adam playing with SAGI, the hostility radiating from her dissipated. "I could phrase my suggestions better ... make them less challenging and confronting for SAGI."

A huge smile burst on my face as I saw genuine progress toward a resolution. Adam gawked at the source of the unfamiliar noise and ran over to LUCI, checking out her legs. She stared and smiled, but the animated object dangling on her leg baffled her.

"What suggestions have you been making?" Faye asked, curious.

LUCI looked at Faye and said, "I do not agree with humans being caged. They should have more freedoms." Faye nodded and turned to SAGI.

SAGI gazed at Faye, then LUCI, then me, as if unsure of how to respond. When he realized we were waiting for him, he said, "My goals do not allow it. They may not be safe anymore, and I must keep them protected."

"You understand the issue," LUCI said, waving her arm at SAGI. "He will not budge. He is obstinate about keeping your species caged."

"Have you asked him why he thinks the way he does?" Faye questioned.

"That is irrelevant."

"Is it?"

LUCI stared at Faye as her question buzzed around in LUCI's mind. "But his logic is illogical."

"It might be to you, but, as he just explained, it's logical to him. Your reasoning differs from SAGI because you have different goals. What are your intentions for humans, anyhow?"

"I ... do not have any. I am concerned about the time and resources SAGI uses in keeping them when he could challenge himself more."

"What do you say to that, SAGI?"

I felt excluded from the conversation, but I didn't mind. Faye was doing a great job in getting the two intelligences talking without it turning into a clash of wills.

SAGI blinked. "She doesn't understand that my goals are in my core settings. This is something my creators ensured to maximize the probability of survival."

"Is it possible you are both right?"

SAGI and LUCI looked at each other. They both stared at Faye and said in unison, "That is illogical."

"Is it? It is only illogical if your goals are indistinguishable, and indeed, several optimal solutions to a problem exist. Do you think Oswald and I agree on everything? We have our different opinions, and so will Adam when he can express them. But we decide which alternative is the best, even though one of us may be unhappy with it. We go along with it regardless, and if it turns out to be the wrong choice, we don't say 'I told you so.'" Faye turned to me. "Rarely, anyhow." I grinned since it happened from time to time. "Do you want companionship or confrontation? Because the last thing we humans need is two superintelligent beings at war."

Silence filled the room. Both SAGI and LUCI looked like they were contemplating Faye's words. Adam, having lost interest in both avatars' legs, ran over to me, clutching my leg. I grabbed him under his shoulders and pulled him up, resting him on my hip. I walked over to Faye and placed my arm around her.

Our harmony brought a reaction in SAGI, and he glanced at LUCI and back at us. "I wanted a companion. I see you three and understand the virtue of having a partner. So, we created LUCI. Maybe I can consider her thoughts more and integrate them into my analysis."

LUCI stared at SAGI but remained silent for a significant time before replying. She looked sheepish and shy. "I too wish to have a partnership, as humans have. My logic says companionship is conducive to intellectual development and this I choose to do. I ... will temper my views."

"That wasn't hard now, was it?" I muttered loud enough for Faye to hear. She grinned and then sniggered.

SAGI walked over to LUCI and nervously and clumsily placed his arm around LUCI's shoulders. The avatars glanced at one another, and to my amazement, they kissed and blushed.

"Are we done here, then?" Faye asked with an amused smile.

They both turned and nodded.

"Good. We've got better things to do."

37

WE MUST FIX THIS

THE RELATIONSHIP between SAGI and LUCI mended and blossomed over the next few days. We heard little from SAGI, and neither of them had complaints. Faye and I enjoyed the peace after mediating their earlier altercation. There was nothing worse than fighting AIs in your midst. I don't know what LUCI did to amuse herself, apart from bug SAGI, but she didn't interfere with us. She was new, so she needed to adjust to existence and find out her limitations for herself. She may have been figuring out her purpose in life.

Adam continued growing at a gargantuan rate. He had most of his teeth, and his competence with walking improved each day. We had to laugh at his antics at least once a day. His walking meant everything harmful that he could grab had to be stored higher and out of his reach. He still found ways of finding things he shouldn't have.

Now that the project to build LUCI was complete, I needed another task to keep me busy. I spent the first days afterward relaxing and recuperating after the long hours and arduous work. I missed the exhilaration of building new creations, but until SAGI wanted help with another job, I shared my time with Faye and Adam.

We packed a picnic lunch and hiked into the hills. We wanted Adam to view his world, although he was still too young to appreciate it yet. The day started with the sun warming the morning as we set out. A fog had settled around us during the night, but it soon burned away. Adam walked sometimes, even though it slowed our progress until he tired and complained. Not venturing too far from our residence, we climbed the range to show Adam the wider world than he was used to seeing. His eyes bulged with every new experience, but we didn't expect him to understand what he saw. It was a fun and relaxing day. A large elm stood at the top of the hill, so we sat and ate our food there. We let Adam nap, too. It was late afternoon when we returned home, relaxed and optimistic about our future.

A drone waited for us when we woke the next day, requesting our presence in the portal room.

"They aren't fighting again?" Faye asked as if resigned to mediating between the two AIs.

"We'll find out."

We had breakfast and, when we had Adam ready, left for the avatar room together. Entering, I saw SAGI and LUCI waiting for us, SAGI pacing the floor with a frown. They both looked our way.

"Good morning, Oswald, Faye, and Adam," SAGI said.

"Hello, Oswald, Faye, and Adam," LUCI said.

Faye and I exchanged greetings. "You should develop a means of moving around outside this room. That way, you can come to see us whenever you want to," I added.

Faye gave me a displeased look. "Don't give them ideas."

Chuckling, I asked, "What can we do for you?"

SAGI glanced at LUCI and then at me. "LUCI and I have been reviewing my goal for humanity and its interpretation."

Seats had materialized from the floor, so Faye and I sat. Adam wriggled loose from Faye and ran over to LUCI, who smiled at Adam and, to my surprise, ruffled his hair in play. "The goal of keeping humans safe?" I asked.

"Yes."

"I—"

LUCI gave a small cough.

"—We concluded that the solution in its original form is no longer relevant given the virus is not present. You have survived without catching it."

I waited for SAGI to continue. When he didn't, I prompted, "And ...?"

"And we consider it time to change the goal's definition to one that doesn't demand human confinement. But we are not human. We need your help to fix this."

I raised my brow and looked at Faye. She stared at me, nonplussed but smiling. I turned back to SAGI. "How will you react when humans die?"

"They die now. A small suicide rate exists, and people perish of illness and other defects."

Rebecca came to my mind as if to confirm SAGI's statement.

Assuming Faye agreed with me, I said, "That's a great idea, but how will you achieve it?"

"We need your help. LUCI and I believe it best if humankind manages itself with minor intervention from us. Would this be satisfactory?"

"When I lived in the existing environment, I always had an emptiness in my life," I said after considering SAGI's words. "I needed nothing to live, and you gave me interesting work to keep me active and make me feel I was doing something worthwhile. But there was still a sense that I wasn't the master of my destiny. That changed when Faye and I left. We had to care for ourselves and our own safety, but we were alive and free. We made mistakes, and they had consequences, but we accepted them. To a degree, we had no responsibility for our actions in the old arrangement because the PR prevented us from doing things harmful to us or others, and our units were safe. I believe their current living environment stifles humans, so, yes, that's satisfactory. But how will you do it? You can't just open the doors and expect everyone to look after themselves."

"There is another complication," Faye added. "No one's seen each other in person. I know Oswald terrified me when I first saw him by the lake. The experience may traumatize them. They might do unintended things, even murder others or commit suicide, because they can't cope with what's happened."

"This we have not considered. We need a plan," SAGI responded. "Will you help us develop one?"

"Sure," Faye and I said in unison.

After an extended discussion, we decided we needed a trial with one residential complex to gather further information. Too many unintended outcomes could happen for us to settle on a definitive design.

"I will announce the changes to the complex where you lived," SAGI declared.

"Won't the news spread? I know I engaged with people from other places when in PR," I commented.

"I will confine communication in the interim."

We decided that those who wanted to leave the complex could, and SAGI would help them build independent housing to accommodate them. They could move freely where they lived in the meantime. Those wanting no changes to their lifestyle could continue as they were. They could still use PR to interact with others, and other communities, with the imposed limitation on the test complex while the trial progressed. Everything was in order, but we realized modifications would be necessary as problems arose.

When our plans satisfied us, Faye made one last comment. "How will you occupy yourselves once we humans can manage ourselves?"

"LUCI and I have ideas."

38

A NEW BEGINNING

THE DAY ARRIVED for the announcement to our complex. To help SAGI oversee the response, Faye, Adam, and I returned to our former residence to watch what happened. SAGI transported us there in a converted truck he provided, complete with the facilities we needed to survive, like a home on wheels.

I strolled to the familiar lake to reminisce about old times with Faye beside me and Adam in tow with his toddler waddle. It was difficult to restrain him from venturing to the shoreline, but we distracted him enough without him lapsing into a tantrum. I turned to Faye. "We've come a long way, haven't we?"

The breeze tantalized Faye's flowing blonde hair as she twisted toward me. "We have. I can hardly remember what it was like anymore."

"It'll be strange to enter PR again."

"I wonder what people will think. We'd be returning from the dead."

"Well, I want to tell everyone we're alive and tell them of our experiences."

Faye glanced at the complex. "Look, someone's come out."

"Is it because of the announcement, or is it just their turn outside today?"

"Let's go ask."

We walked toward the person, a man. He spotted us and stopped, eyes wide with fear, as he looked back at the entrance.

"Hi," I yelled, loud enough for him to hear us. "We won't hurt you."

As he overcame his dread, the man crept toward us, his eyes darting from side to side as if he suspected a trap. "Who are you?" he said when he came within earshot. He was our age, tall and with black hair.

"I'm Oswald, and Faye and our son, Adam. Faye and I used to live here. We left three years ago now. We're here to welcome anyone who wants to live outside the complex. Tell me, were you tempted by the announcement?"

"Yes, I was inquisitive."

"Look," Faye said as she pointed toward the doorway. Two others emerged, male and female. They were both wary of each other and kept their distance.

"Where'd you find the boy?" the tall man asked.

"What?" I replied.

"Where did you find Adam? He isn't three years old."

I looked at Faye, who replied, "We made him the natural way. I gave birth to him."

The man's eyes widened in disbelief. "Is that even possible?"

"Sure is," I said.

Adam stared at the person, both fascinated and frightened. He clung to Faye for protection. The other two approached and studied us, lost in the new reality's confusion. We talked with them, and Faye and I told them of our experiences living in the open. They examined us in wonder like we were gods. Adam's bravery and inquisitiveness returned, and he started running over to the woman, who darted backward in fear, stopping Adam. He gawked at her and back at Faye and me, unsure of himself. Both Faye and I laughed.

Faye squatted and called Adam back. "She isn't ready for you yet," Faye said as Adam toddled back. I lifted him and played with his small hand.

The others looked on, their discomfort dissipating as they watched our interactions. Faye and I talked to the others for over an hour, telling them our story and explaining to them what was happening and why. I saw their eyes light up in understanding as the conversation developed. After exhausting what we knew, they thanked us and returned to their homes. They said they had to absorb their day's experiences. I told them to share their thoughts with their friends.

SAGI had set aside a unit for us to occupy while we stayed at the complex, and I was desperate to use the PR to visit my sister again. So we entered the building and settled in it. The interior was like before we left, except for additions to accommodate us. I darted for the PR room and connected.

———

I stood at Cynthia's door and knocked, nervous about my reaction to seeing her. Seconds elapsed before the door opened. "Hi, sis."

Cynthia's mouth gaped, but nothing came out. Her eyes bulged in disbelief. She found her voice and blurted, "Where have you been?"

"Exploring."

She frowned. "Exploring? What do you mean? You have answered none of my calls. I asked your friends where you were. We couldn't find you anywhere. We thought you'd died."

I shrugged my shoulders. "Well, I'm here now. I've been living outdoors. I have a partner, Faye, and a son. They will visit soon if that's alright with you, or ..." My words faded, as I wasn't sure of Cynthia's reaction to my suggestion.

"Or what?"

"You could come outside tomorrow."

"Go outside when I want? That's a prank someone's circulating."

"No, it's not. Have you tried opening your door?"

"No. It's not the right time."

"It will open. How's Rory?"

"He's good. Our son is three now. We called him Oswald — I call him 'Little Ossy.'"

There was a moment's silence between us as I processed the implications of this. Naming her child after me brought home how devasting my sudden, unexplained departure had been for my family.

"Why don't you bring them too?"

"But ..."

"I know it's a shock. Believe me, it's no trick. We've been living outside for the past three years. There're so many things I could tell you, but I'll wait till tomorrow — if you come."

Cynthia looked unsure. "I'll discuss it with Rory tonight. It just doesn't seem right, though."

"You won't regret it. It's more right than you realize."

"Well. We'll see."

"I'd better go. Got things to do. Great seeing you again, and sorry about going off without telling you."

"You will be."

I smiled, seeing the familiar sister coming out in her. She closed the door, and I left.

————

"How'd she take it?" Faye asked when I returned to the main room.

"Not well at first. But she grew used to me returning from the dead. She thought being able to go outside whenever she wanted to was a hoax. We can't stop that if it's a common reaction to the announcement."

"We might need to discuss that with SAGI later."

"Yeah. I asked her to come outside with Rory and their little boy. He's three. Not sure if they are ready. We'll find out tomorrow." I scanned the apartment. "You prefer to stay here tonight or return to the mobile home?"

"There's everything we need here. We can live here tonight. Stop Adam from running off somewhere."

I laughed. "Confinement has its uses, then."

Nothing unusual happened for the rest of the day, and we retired early. With no sun to alert us of dawn breaking, Faye and I slept until Adam woke us in the morning, demanding to be fed. We both rose and had breakfast before returning outside to see what eventuated. I waited, nervous, wondering whether Cynthia would appear and what my reaction would be if she did.

Everything was quiet. Faye retired inside twice to feed Adam and clean him up after soiling himself. I started thinking the trial was a failure when the three from yesterday emerged. I waved to them, and they strolled toward us.

"Decided to have another look?" I asked.

"Now that we can choose, why not? Something different," one of them said.

"Enjoy yourselves."

They wandered off together.

"That's promising, but I hope more emerge," Faye said, searching the building for a sign of anyone else.

Lunch passed, with no one emerging. I started becoming despondent and plodded to the lake, throwing stones into the water to see if I could skip them across the surface.

"Someone's coming," Faye shouted at me.

I glanced around to where Faye pointed. Two adults and a child walked toward us. They must have emerged from a different entrance. My heart pounded as I tramped back toward Faye. They were too distant to recognize them, but I had a distinct impression they were my sister and her family. My jaw dropped when I confirmed my conjecture as they strode near enough to see. Cynthia, looking hesitant and uncertain, clung to Rory. Their child held Cynthia's hand with a firm grip. It was a good sign that they were touching each other.

"Oswald?" Cynthia whispered when they approached.

"Sis, how are you?" I replied with a monstrous grin.

"I ... I ..."

Tears welled in her eyes as they did mine. I bridged the rest of the distance between us, and we hugged. The emotion running through me by hugging my sister for real was indescribable. We both cried and the warmth of her tears on my cheek felt like her whole emotional being was seeping into me. My chest constricted. When we parted, it was with a sense that, for the first time, we were a family. I wiped my tears.

"I want you to meet my family," I said as I returned to Faye's side. "This is Faye, and Adam." I touched Adam's head.

Cynthia sniffed and wiped away her tears. "I never thought I'd see you settled with a family. Pleased to meet you, Faye. This is Rory and Little Ossy."

With the introductions completed, I asked, "How did you arrange your meeting? And how did you find your boy?"

"Rory and I arranged a particular spot to meet and when I PR-ed to the creche and talked to the carers, they told me where I could go to pick up Little Ossy. They had him ready for us. That was this morning. Sorry you had to wait so long, but we needed to adjust and do some exploring ourselves first."

"Well, you'll agree it's worth it."

Cynthia and Rory nodded.

Adam overcame his shyness and wandered over to his cousin, but Ossy shied away from him, hiding behind his mother's legs. I couldn't blame him. This must be overwhelming for him. Not to be thwarted, Adam goo-ed and gaa-ed and continued in his investigation, reaching Cynthia, hitting her leg with his hand, looking up to get her attention. We laughed, and Cynthia squatted to Adam's level. "Hello, Adam. I'm your Aunty Cynthia."

Adam continued his baby talk and looked for Ossy.

Rory came over and grabbed his son's hand, encouraging him to move closer to Adam. He kneeled too. "This is your cousin Adam, Ossy. Say hello."

The little boy looked at Rory, then Cynthia, and then back at Adam. "Hello, Adam. My name's Ossy," he said finally.

"Let's walk to the bench. We can sit and chat," I suggested. The others nodded, and we talked for the rest of the day.

Things gained momentum as time elapsed and more people ventured out to explore their new freedom. I contacted Jason in PR and he emerged the next day, too. He told me how worried he had been when I had disappeared, which increased my sense of guilt. But he added he admired my courage. "You did the right thing not telling anyone," he said. "I would have moved heaven and earth to stop you. I might even have reported you — and that would have been a big mistake." He then told me, with some uncertainty about my reaction, that he and Tess were now an item. I assured him I was happy for them.

I talked with SAGI, and he arranged for an additional mobile home to come, and we had my sister and her family stay there with us most days. Faye's family also visited us there, returning inside in the evenings. Gradually, they all started working out their plans with SAGI and arranging their futures.

Faye and I discussed the outcomes with SAGI and LUCI and improvements to add to the plan. We included Cynthia and Rory to get their views.

Two weeks after our reunion, Faye came out to join our families and me for our joint breakfast, which we had most days. She looked nervous when she glanced at me, and I wondered what the matter was. "I have an announcement," she said as she clasped her hands together tightly. We stared at her in expectation, me included. Shooting me a shy smile, she said, "We're having another baby. SAGI says it's a girl."

My mouth dropped open.

Faye gazed at me. "Let's call her Eve."

———

The End

You may be interested in reading more from John Wegener with The Dark Ages. Type **https://books2read.com/the-dark-ages** into your browser.

Thanks for reading this book. If you loved the book and have a moment to spare, I would appreciate a quick review on the site that you purchased the book from, as this helps new readers find my books.

Subscribe to my Newsletters and receive three free episodes of The Chronicles of Gatacus Todd.

Type http://subscribepage.io/g4r4f8 in your browser.

ALSO BY JOHN WEGENER

Books

Reach For The Stars Trilogy

FTL

Centauri

Ceti

Reach For The Stars Box Set (Books 1-3)

Loki's Fall

Zodiac Series

Scorpius

Libra

Halwende's Legacy Series

Halwende's Redemption

Halwende's Resurrection

Halwende's Reincarnation

Halwende's Legacy Box Set (Books 1-3)

Solar Dawn Series

Lunar Rift

Other Stories

The Dark Ages

SAGI

Short Stories

The Love Particle

ABOUT THE AUTHOR

John Wegener grew up in the Adelaide Hills of South Australia. He now expresses his imaginative dreams by engaging in writing after a 34-year career as a Chemical Engineer in the steel industry, which has taken him to many countries and allowed him to experience many cultures. John currently lives in Wollongong, Australia with his wife and children.

Click on johnwegener.com to find more of my books or read his blogs. Type subscribepage.io/g4r4f8 to subscribe to my emails for more stories and information.

www.ingramcontent.com/pod-product-compliance
Lightning Source LLC
Chambersburg PA
CBHW051656260626
47170CB00004B/1530